Praise

"A wonderful, e...
story ab...
—*RT Book Revi*...

"Lois Richer delivers a touching, evocative,
wonderful story of selfless love."
—*RT Book Reviews* on *A Cowboy's Honor*

"Lois Richer's *His Winter Rose* is a wonderful,
warm love story with two powerful
protagonists."
—*RT Book Reviews*

Praise for Allie Pleiter

"Delightful and clever, this first novel
is worth reading."
—*Library Journal* on *Bad Heiress Day*

"Pleiter delivers an appealing romance as well
as a story filled with interesting characters."
—*RT Book Reviews* on *Bluegrass Courtship*

"Allie Pleiter has written a sweet
and tenderly moving story."
—*RT Book Reviews* on *Bluegrass Hero*

LOIS RICHER

likes variety. From her time in human resources management to entrepreneurship, life has held plenty of surprises. "Having given up on fairy tales, I was happily involved in building a restaurant when a handsome prince walked into my life and upset all my career plans with a wedding ring. Motherhood quickly followed. I guess the seeds of my storytelling took root because of two small boys who kept demanding 'Then what, Mom?' The miracle of God's love for His children, the blessing of true love, the joy of sharing Him with others—that is a story that can be told a thousand ways and yet still be brand-new." Lois Richer intends to go right on telling it.

ALLIE PLEITER

Enthusiastic but slightly untidy mother of two, RITA® Award finalist Allie Pleiter writes both fiction and nonfiction. An avid knitter and unreformed chocoholic, she spends her days writing books, drinking coffee and finding new ways to avoid housework. Allie grew up in Connecticut, holds a BS in Speech from Northwestern University and spent fifteen years in the field of professional fundraising. She lives with her husband, children and a Havanese dog named Bella in the suburbs of Chicago, Illinois.

Easter Promises
Lois Richer
Allie Pleiter

Steeple
Hill®

Published by Steeple Hill Books™

STEEPLE HILL BOOKS

Steeple Hill®

ISBN-13: 978-0-373-87584-9

Recycling programs for this product may not exist in your area.

EASTER PROMISES

CONTENTS

DESERT ROSE

Lois Richer

This book is dedicated to Pastor Dan as thanks for his revealing study of the Psalms.

But when I am afraid, I will put my confidence in you. Yes, I will trust the promises of God. And since I am trusting him, what can mere man do to me?
—*Psalms* 56: 3, 4

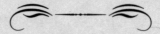

Chapter One

"My client has decided not to make an offer on your floral business."

Jayne Rose thanked the Realtor and hung up, but her stomach churned with angst.

Lord, how am I going to help Granny Em?

The shop's doorbell interrupted her silent plea. She shoved the sturdy frames of her glasses an inch higher on her nose and peered through the thick lenses at her newest customer.

"Welcome to Rose's Roses. Can I help you?"

"I'm not sure," the man said. "Your window display intrigued me. I'm kind of a window shopper."

"Ah." *I don't have time,* Jayne thought.

"I'm thinking Easter lilies," he mused. "A friend loves spring, though the Palm Springs version isn't exactly what she was used to in England."

"Well, it's a bit early for potted Easter lilies," Jayne explained. "But I could make up an arrangement." She grabbed an order form. "Name?"

"Well, I'm not sure…" He peered at the orchids Jayne had

unpacked late last night. "Those are amazing. Maybe I should—"

"Would you like a minute?" she offered with a desperate glance at the clock.

"At least a minute," he agreed, but his gaze rested on her.

"I'll finish some errands while you decide. Call when you're ready." Jayne stepped inside the cooler, anxious to finish her wedding order.

But she couldn't dismiss the man in the shop so easily. Through the glass walls she saw him perusing her stock. He was tall and lean, muscular, but not bulky. His dark brown eyes studied the bucket of roses intently while he tilted back on his heels. Jayne immediately labeled him artistic, though she couldn't have explained why. Perhaps it was the easy way he moved, as if he was totally comfortable with himself.

Jayne had never managed to achieve that ease, not since the accident.

Stop staring and concentrate. She consulted her list. Everything was almost ready for delivery, only a few more tweaks. She'd barely finished gathering what she needed when the shop's bell rang again.

So he'd left. She ignored her disappointment and took her time selecting the best blooms. Even though the money she'd make on this wedding was minimal, Jayne believed every bride deserved a beautiful wedding. Just because this bride didn't have a lot of money didn't mean Rose's Roses would skimp.

She had one foot out of the cooler when she heard voices.

"Jayne's the most perfect florist. I'm not like her other clients, you know. I haven't got a bundle of cash to spend on my wedding, but Jayne doesn't care. She pours her soul into everything she does. I'll hate it if this place has to close."

Jayne grinned at the glowing tribute. LouAnne was such a

sweetheart. Jayne stepped around the corner with a smile on her lips and saw LouAnne talking to her earlier customer.

"Hey, Jayne," LouAnne said.

"Hey, yourself. Aren't you supposed to be at home, dressing in all that ivory and lace?" For a minute Jayne worried LouAnne was having bridal jitters. She censured the thought. LouAnne was committed and confident. Her marriage would be solid and happy.

Jayne quashed a rush of longing to be in love like that.

"I would be dressing," LouAnne said, "but I just found out my bridesmaid wrecked her gown. Now she's wearing green instead of blue. Can we change the ribbons in the flowers?"

Jayne stifled a groan. Changes at this stage meant even more time spent on a not very profitable order, which was okay, but there was still that quilter's convention tomorrow to prepare for.

"I'm asking too much of you." LouAnne's pretty face fell.

"Of course you're not. You go home. I'll handle everything," Jayne said, pushing LouAnne toward the door. "Move it, lady, or you'll be late for your own wedding. I'll have everything at the church before you get there."

"See what I mean? She's a blessing," LouAnne said over one shoulder to the man who stood watching them. She paused long enough to hug Jayne. Then she hurried away, glowing with the radiance of a bride-to-be.

"It's not going to be quite as simple as you said, is it?" His quiet question broke the silence.

"It will be very not-simple," Jayne agreed. "But it will happen." She began the delicate process of unweaving the blue ribbon from the arrangement she'd just finished.

"Can I help?" he offered. "I promise I'll try my best not to wreck your flowers."

"I'm sure you don't want—"

"I'd really like to help, if you'll allow me." The firm

response combined with the rich glow of his dark brown eyes sent a powerful message. "By the way, I'm Ben. Ben Cummings." He held out a hand.

"Jayne Rose," she said as his strong fingers enclosed hers.

"Of Rose's Roses." He grinned.

He really was the most handsome man. Sprinkles of sunlight dappled the sandy strands that flopped across his forehead and framed those amazing eyes, brown with a capital *B*. He wore knee-length shorts and a polo shirt and both of them fit like a custom-tailored glove, as elegant as any Hollywood visitor to Palm Springs.

"Let me help, Jayne."

She thought about it for two seconds. Help was good. Help was exactly what she'd been praying for.

"If you're sure?" She felt dubious about his abilities.

"I am sure."

"Then I'm grateful. Here, you lift it out like this."

He watched for a moment then nodded. "Got it."

Normally Jayne wouldn't dream of allowing a customer to help, but desperate times called for innovative solutions and with her assistant absent, she was frantic for help.

As Ben patiently coaxed the ribbon free, Jayne decided he was better at it than she was, probably because she felt so rushed. She had to stop reworking the bridal bouquet twice to help customers.

"Is it always so busy around here?" he asked when the customers had left.

"Mmm. Look, Mr. Cummings, do—"

"Call me Ben. No, I don't have to be anywhere and yes, I really want to help."

"Okay," she said with a smile. "Then I appreciate it. I only hope my grandmother arrives soon. I need the van to deliver these."

"Is she making other deliveries?"

"No. My grandmother, Emma Rose, is the owner of Rose's Roses. She's supposed to be at home, resting. But she insisted on coming in this afternoon, so I had to send my assistant to pick her up. Emma can't drive anymore."

"One too many accidents, huh?" Amusement underlay his words.

"Not exactly." Jayne set aside the sheaf of cascading pink roses. "Emma hasn't been well."

"You call her by her first name?"

"At work, yes. It just seems more…businesslike." She studied him. "How are you doing?"

"Finished this one. I'm guessing there's another to match it?"

He was quick. And good. Not one stem had been broken. Ben Cummings was a lifesaver.

"There are two more in the cooler," Jayne said. "I'll get them."

Ben rejected that and carried the big vases out by himself. Working swiftly but carefully, he extricated the blue ribbons.

"Why does your friend think you might have to close Rose's Roses?" he asked, watching as she replaced the ribbons he'd removed with green ones.

"Emma's trying to sell. Or at least find a partner." In any other circumstance Jayne would have died before sharing such personal details. But the frustration of not finding a buyer for Rose's Roses had her stressed out. "Emma needs an operation. Her insurance won't cover it."

"Oh." He left it open for her to decide whether to explain or not.

Jayne needed to talk to someone. Why not a total stranger?

"I was twelve when my parents died and I came to live with Grandma Em. We don't have anyone else. Emma wanted to be sure that if something happened to her, I'd be taken care of, so she reduced her own health insurance to buy a life insurance policy to benefit me."

"That was a while ago?"

"Yes," Jayne admitted. "Twelve years. I didn't realize she hadn't changed her plan back until her health got worse and I took over the bookkeeping."

"That's a big responsibility."

"I'm good with math." She sighed, remembering the shock. "It's ironic. Emma didn't increase her health insurance at that time because she was saving to buy out her partner and be independent. I guess she felt money was too tight to waste on insurance she'd never use. She's always been so healthy. But now she needs a partner."

"Or a buyer."

"Yes." The worry of losing Emma gnawed a new hole in Jayne's stomach. She had to find a way to pay for that operation. Emma's heart wouldn't hold on forever and Jayne wasn't about to lose the last of her family.

"I'm finished with these vases."

"Thank you very much." She glanced at the clock. Time was fleeting and still no van. *God?*

"Why don't you buy your grandmother out?" he asked. "It looks like you enjoy this work."

"I love it," Jayne said fiercely. "I'd like nothing better than to buy Rose's Roses. But I haven't got the money and no one will lend it to me. For some reason, you have to have money to borrow it." She checked the clock again. "I wish they'd get here. The wedding's in an hour. This stuff should already be at the church."

"You can borrow my car. It's not a van, but it's big enough to fit the vases, I think." Ben nodded toward the black SUV parked by the curb. "Fortunately, it's empty at the moment. I've been hauling stuff," he explained.

"Oh?"

"I was trying to landscape." He made a face. "I'm lousy at it."

The word *landscape* tweaked her interest, but Jayne ignored it. She picked up the phone and dialed. Her grandmother didn't have a cell phone, but her assistant, Sidney, did.

"Hi. Where are you? I've got to get this wedding order—"

"We're stuck in traffic. There was an accident."

"Is Granny all right?" Panic rose like a tidal wave.

"She's fine. The accident's in front of us. We're going to be awhile."

"Okay, I'll think of something else. Bye." Jayne hung up, squeezed her eyes closed and prayed for help.

The sound of keys rattling startled her.

"Take them and go deliver your stuff," Ben said, brown eyes crinkling at the corners. "I can hold down the fort here for a few minutes. Or, I'll drive you—if you'd rather not leave me here alone."

It was so tempting.

"Come on. I've got the motor running, so the air-conditioning should have things cooled down. Let's get loading."

It was obvious her van would not arrive in time. Jayne studied Ben Cummings. Had God sent her help via him?

"A really bad guy wouldn't offer you his car keys," he teased.

"Are you sure about this?"

"Positive," he said with a smile. "Shall I load this vase?"

She nodded. Accepting Ben Cummings's help seemed presumptuous and too easy, but it also seemed like an answer to a prayer.

She turned away to load corsages and bouquets into a flat box. Ben carried that out, along with the rest of the order while Jayne hurried to the back of the building to retrieve her special surprise for LouAnne.

But when she tried to lift one of the two small cedar trees she'd draped in white tulle and tied with a white satin bow, it was too heavy. How on earth had Sidney manhandled the trees in here?

"Jayne?"

"Back here." She pushed even harder, struggling to slide the tree forward. It refused to budge. She stepped backward and bumped into Ben.

"Trouble?" His hand steadied her.

"I guess I shouldn't have watered them this morning," Jayne mumbled, embarrassed at her clumsiness. She edged away from him, winced as her shin collided with a pail of water. "Now they're too heavy. I'll have to leave them behind." Frustration gnawed at her.

"What are they for?"

"I wanted to place one on either side of the entry. The church is small and rather plain. I thought there should be something to announce that a wonderful wedding is about to take place."

"That was generous of you."

She caught a glimpse of the clock on the wall and shook her head. "Never mind."

"Could I drive around to the back? Load them from here?"

"Maybe." Jayne explained how to access the rear door. Moments later Ben had backed in and was rearranging things in his vehicle. Then another man appeared and the two of them lifted the little trees with no difficulty.

"Thanks a lot," Ben said to the guy, who saluted before walking away. "Ready to go?" he asked Jayne.

"I guess." He made everything seem so simple.

"You realize I'll have to go with you? There's no way you'll be able to unload those trees yourself. Can you lock up?"

She dialed Sidney.

"I'm taking the flowers to the church. Has Emma got her keys?" A pause for confirmation and Jayne hung up. She clicked the lock on the front door. "They're still stuck in traffic. You're sure you want to do this?"

"It'll be fun." He grinned at her dubious look. "Oh ye of little faith."

So he knew some Scripture. Granny Em would like him.

Ben Cummings was a good driver and they arrived at the church with no trouble. While he found a helper to unload the trees, Jayne began decorating the church. Fortunately, only the minister had arrived early.

"This is the last of them." Ben placed the two large vases where she directed. Following her lead, he began hanging pew bows, laughed when she bumped into him on the last row.

"I'm no wedding expert, but shouldn't the place have been decorated last night?"

"There was a funeral." Jayne pretended her face wasn't fire-red and scanned the sanctuary with a satisfied look. "It looks pretty good, don't you think?"

"I think your friend will be ecstatic. You've turned ordinary into a bride's dream, and done it very tastefully. Will you have to come back later for the trees?"

"No. I'm leaving them. The exterior could use a bit of green." Jayne adjusted the candles on the altar before pulling out her camera and snapping pictures. "I keep an album so future brides can see what's possible."

"Very smart. I agree with your friend. It would be a pity if Rose's Roses had to close."

"Thanks." The deflation that always fell after delivering a bridal order hit Jayne as they walked to the car. Would she ever get to be a bride?

Who would want to marry a clumsy, half-blind woman with scars?

"Thank you for pitching in the way you did. I don't know how I would have managed without you."

"My pleasure." Ben began explaining about his recent arrival in Palm Springs. It seemed moments later that they pulled up in front of the shop. "Have you time for a coffee?"

In that moment, Jayne realized she wanted to know more about Ben Cummings. About his job. His life. It would be wonderful to sit in the sun and share conversation with a handsome man. But there was always work.

Besides, Jayne had no idea how to go on a date.

"I—I can't. Thank you for asking, but I've got a convention booked for tomorrow. There's a banquet in the evening and I need to do the table centerpieces." Jayne grasped the door handle, paused before opening it. "I can't tell you how much I appreciate your help. Will you allow me to send a bouquet to your friend at no charge?"

"Certainly not." Ben seemed annoyed by the suggestion. "You need to learn to accept a gift, Jayne Rose, when it's a gesture of friendliness."

"I only wanted to return the favor you did," she murmured quietly. She slid her fingers over the door panel, searching for the handle. "Thanks again. Goodbye."

"Wait."

Jayne froze. Ever since the accident that had turned her life upside down, she'd felt like an odd man out. Changing schools, listening to other girls talk about boys, dates and fashion when she was still learning how to walk without a limp, when the scars on her arms were still ugly and rippled and everyone gawked. Jayne had tried to join in, but no one saw *her,* only her injuries. Now the wretched feelings of being an oddball came rushing back.

Ben had seemed interested in talking to her. But maybe he was simply being polite. Jayne knew she wasn't like other girls. Since she'd changed schools, she'd never belonged to the "in" group. She'd never achieved the kind of easy camaraderie she'd had before the accident, certainly never with a man.

And yet with Ben she'd felt comfortable.

"Jayne?"

"Yes?" Where *was* the door handle?

"I'm sorry. I was rude." He grasped her chin, coaxed her to look at him. "As a matter of fact, there is a favor I need."

"Oh." Suspicion raised its head. Jayne frowned, jerking her chin away. "What?"

"I bought a house here in Palm Springs. A fixer-upper they called it." He smiled as if that was funny. "The inside work is finally done. That's not the problem."

"Uh-huh."

"It's the yard. I want to landscape it, but clearly I have no idea how to do that in this climate. I've killed everything I've brought home," he said mournfully.

"And the favor?"

"Do you know anyone who could help me? Preferably someone who knows desert plants, tolerances and such."

Jayne's heart thudded an extra beat. "I know someone," she replied.

"Who?"

"Me. Landscaping is where I'd hoped to go next with Rose's Roses. If I could get a loan, I'd expand into that field." She got caught up in her dreams and began talking about her favorite subject until muffled laughter finally stopped her. She grimaced. "Sorry. Sometimes I get carried away."

"That's not a bad thing." His smile raised butterflies in her stomach.

"I guess," Jayne murmured, averting her eyes. "What kind of landscape?"

"Something unusual."

"I can do unusual." She bit her lip and decided to take a risk. "I'd appreciate a chance to bid on the job."

"Don't say that until you see the scope of it," Ben warned.

"When?" she asked eagerly.

"Tomorrow afternoon?"

"Great. What's the address?" Jayne scribbled it down with the pen he handed her. "One-thirty? I go to church in the morning with Emma. The one we just decorated, actually."

"One-thirty is fine. Thanks, Jayne."

"Thank you. Bye." She wiggled out of his vehicle, slammed the door shut and hurried into the shop, ignoring the twinge of pain in her bad knee.

Finally, a job she could sink her teeth into. Maybe the only landscaping job she would ever have if she didn't soon find someone to buy the business.

Gran's not getting any better, God.

Dreaming of being a bride? Jayne had no time for that. She needed to concentrate on the issue at hand and get the money for Emma's operation.

And she needed to get it soon.

Chapter Two

The little brown church stood proudly in the sunlight on Sunday morning, the two trees, now bare of their wedding tulle, guarding its front doors.

Ben stepped under the porticoed entrance, hoping the church was big enough to hold one more. Judging by the number of cars in the lot, this church was popular.

"Hi." A tiny woman in lilac handed him a bulletin. "I'm Emma Rose," she said softly, her breathing uneven. "Welcome to First Avenue Church. The service is just about to start."

"Thank you," he murmured. Jayne's grandmother. They shared the same amazing turquoise eyes. Ben took the seat the usher led him to and scanned the congregation.

Jayne sat near the front, her beautiful auburn curls bunched on top of her head, glasses teetering precariously on the end of her nose as she leaned over to hug a young girl seated beside her. In fact, there was a whole row of young girls. Was Jayne a Sunday school teacher?

His curiosity about this woman bordered on the ridiculous. Ben thought about her constantly, about how hard she'd worked to make that wedding just right. He thought about the confident way she moved around the shop, snatching up this and that and forming them into something beautiful, only stumbling when she became self-conscious. He thought about how her hair had glistened a deep ruby when the sun caught it, about the scars he'd glimpsed on her forearms, and about the way she sometimes nibbled on her full bottom lip.

The chords of the old organ startled Ben into attention as the congregation rose for prayer. The service began with Jayne's group of girls playing a handbell selection that echoed to the rafters like some wordless heavenly choir. The rest of the service wasn't overly long, but there was a lot packed into it. Prayers for members who were missing due to illness, hymns sung with gusto and joy, words of encouragement and teaching to remind that God truly cared about even the smallest details. By the time the last chord died and people rose to leave, Ben's heart had been refreshed. He decided he'd come here again. He'd make this church his home, for now.

He turned to leave.

"What are you doing here?" Jayne blocked his way out of the pew, turquoise eyes swirling with confusion. "I thought I was to meet you at your place, at one-thirty." She peered at her watch.

"You are. But I'm new in town and I wanted to attend services. I thought this might be a good church to visit. I was right." He smiled at her, surprised by how young she looked with her gorgeous hair pulled back off her face. "Have you attended here for a long time, Jayne?"

"Since I came to live with Granny." She blinked at her grandmother, who had moved near. "Emma, this is Ben Cummings. He helped me with the wedding yesterday. This is my grandmother, Ben. Emma Rose."

"I'm glad to meet you." Her delicate hand felt frail against his and she seemed to sway slightly. "Are you all right, ma'am?"

"I'm fine." The tiny woman wheezed breathily. "Though you are handsome enough to make a lady swoon. Ben, did you say?" she said as she studied him.

"Ben Cummings, Miss Emma." He bowed in his most gallant manner, hoping to impress, though he had a hunch Emma was as sharp as a tack and wouldn't be easily fooled. "At your service."

"Are you indeed?" A hint of something edged her words, but a moment later, Emma's smile returned. "Did you enjoy our service, Ben?"

"Very much. Would you two ladies join me for lunch?" The words emerged of their own accord, but Ben wasn't taking them back. It would be fun to shed his solitary status for a while and share a meal.

"I don't—"

"What a lovely idea!" Emma said, cutting off her grand-daughter's protest. "Jayne and I would enjoy it very much."

Jayne didn't look delighted, but Ben ignored that. He'd spent most of last evening thinking about Jayne Rose instead of working on his novel. Today he intended to find some answers to his many questions about her.

"How about we meet at…" Ben named a restaurant he'd eaten at before. "Or I could drive you both there, if that's easier."

"We'll meet you." Jayne avoided looking at him.

"Great. I'll go get a table. Do you have a preference?"

"No." Jayne moved to speak to someone else. Ben wondered if she was annoyed.

"My granddaughter tells me you need a landscaper." Emma sat down. Her lack of color frightened him.

"Yes." He debated a moment. "Are you truly all right, Miss Emma?"

"I just need a minute to catch my breath." She tilted her head back, closed her eyes and began a deep breathing routine.

Ben caught Jayne studying them. She disappeared. A few moments later she returned and touched Emma's arm.

"The van's at the door, Grandmother. Are you sure you want to go out for lunch?" she asked, her voice soft.

"Perhaps not today." Emma struggled to rise.

Ben assisted her and kept his arm under her hand as they left the church.

"May we make it another time, Ben?"

"We must." He helped her into the van. "I hope you feel better soon."

"Thank you, Ben." Emma waggled her fingers goodbye.

"I'll be at your house at one-thirty, as agreed," Jayne said before she pulled away.

"I'm looking forward to it," Ben murmured.

And he was.

Jayne pressed the button at the security gates and waited for an answer. Ben Cummings lived here? The place resembled a 1950s hideaway for some legendary movie star. Palm Springs was certainly known for that.

Once she'd been buzzed in, Jayne felt her fears rising. The yard was huge. She didn't have a crew. There was a lot of work to be done. Doubt escalated.

"Are you staying in your car?" Ben, with those delicious brown eyes, stood waiting.

"No." Reluctantly she opened the car door and stepped out carefully, favoring her knee. Then she leaned back in for her sketch pad and pencil.

"Welcome to my home," he said.

"Thanks."

Ben kept talking, but Jayne didn't hear. She surveyed the yard. As she did, a low buzz of creativity in her brain began building to a crescendo.

"Boundless possibilities," she murmured as she sketched.

"Excuse me?"

"I need a few minutes." She wandered away, trying not to limp. If only she hadn't worn heels this morning. Her knee always rebelled against heels, but her soul loved the elegant feel of them. She didn't often feel elegant.

Jayne paused here and there for perspective before continuing around the site. A boulder nested against a shady bit of fence. She sat down to rest her leg, her fingers rippling ideas across page after page. Sometime later Ben's voice penetrated.

"Care for some lemonade?"

"Thank you." She sipped thirstily. A soft wind blew off the desert, tousled her hair and rustled a nearby palm. "It's warm for February."

"By the time Easter gets here it'll be gorgeous." Ben leaned against a palm tree, watching her with those dark brooding eyes.

"Can I ask you some questions?"

He frowned, but finally nodded.

"Do you intend to use this space for entertaining?"

"No. The more privacy the better." Blunt but definite.

"Do you want flowers?" She studied him closely. "Will you have a gardener?"

"No gardener. Just me."

So he didn't have a wife?

"I want whatever is carefree and drought tolerant."

"May I see inside the house?"

"Why?" His brows lowered darkly.

"I'm not prying," she assured him. "I need to see the vistas from inside and get a feel for the transition. You don't want visitors to be jolted when they step inside."

"I don't have visitors." But after a moment Ben led the way to the front door and pushed it open.

Her curiosity growing, Jayne stepped through the doorway

and stopped, surprised by the decor. It was homey and relaxing. Luxurious, yet not overdone. She kept walking, but each room read the same—comfortable anonymity. Who was Ben Cummings?

The study overlooked the front yard. Here she found a bit of his personality in the masses of books filling mahogany shelves, many of them by the same author—David Bentley. Ben had more than one copy of the same titles.

"You must be a fan of this Bentley fellow," she mused.

"Mmm." Noncommittal.

"This is where you work?"

"Yes."

"What do you do?" The space was lovely, but quite impersonal. Jayne needed something of Ben's taste to go on.

"I manage assets," Ben answered after an overlong silence.

"Oh." Jayne wrinkled her nose. "I don't know much about that." She saw more books lined up next to the window. "You really like reading."

"Yes."

He shifted from one foot to the other. Clearly he didn't like her being here. Jayne moved to the window. A fountain perhaps? Cactus certainly.

"Are you finished?"

She blinked back to awareness. "What? Oh. Yes. Thanks."

"How long will it take you to come up with an idea?" He followed her to the front door.

"I already have ideas, but I need time to put them together." And figure out how to get a crew and a way to pay them. "A week?"

"Fine." Ben walked beside her to her car. "Anything else?"

"Budget?" She blinked at the amount. "And are there specific materials or plants, furniture, you want?"

"I want to be able to comfortably sit out here and watch

the sunsets without someone watching me. Beyond that…" He shrugged.

Ben's repeated request for privacy puzzled Jayne, but one didn't question a would-be client. She closed her notebook.

"Okay, I'll get to work. Oh." She whirled around, found him too near and backed up a step, wobbling just a bit. "I left my glass—"

"Your glasses are on your nose." He grinned.

"I meant my lemonade glass." Her cheeks burned.

"I'll get it later." He moved slightly closer. "Can I ask *you* a question?"

"I guess."

"Those glasses look very cumbersome. Why don't you wear contacts?"

"I told you my parents died?" Jayne waited for his nod. "It was a car accident. I was in the car. One of my injuries was to my head—optic nerve injuries. Contacts aren't an option."

"I'm sorry," he said quietly.

"It's okay." She debated how much to explain. "For years the doctors said there was nothing they could do."

"And now?"

"My ophthalmologist says there's a new operation I could have."

"But?"

"It's incredibly risky," she murmured. "There aren't any guarantees."

"There never are in life."

"I manage." Indignant, Jayne stood taller. "I also have scars on my arms. And I hurt my knee, too, so I'm clumsy sometimes and bump into things. But I've learned to cope."

Ben said nothing.

"Anyway…" She paused awkwardly.

"You're looking for an investor for Rose's Roses."

"Or a partner. Ideally, I'd love to buy it, but…" She shrugged.

"The money issue."

"Yeah." Jayne wondered if he was worried about her ability to complete his job. "Any work I took on here would be finished regardless of what happens with Rose's Roses."

"I'm sure it would, Jayne. I never thought otherwise." His smile made those espresso eyes melt. "I recall a friend who started his business with help from a not-for-profit group called Restart that lends money. You could apply to them. Wait a minute. I think I have some information in my office." Ben left and returned to hand her some papers. "Maybe Restart would help you, too."

"Why are you doing this?" she asked.

"Someone had faith in me once. I'd like to pass it on."

"Well, thank you." Jayne studied the loan papers while trying to ignore her heart's bump of hope. No point in dreaming. She still didn't have the down payment she'd need for a loan.

"My card's attached. Call me when you your bid is ready."

"I will. Thanks for the opportunity." There was nothing else to say. As Jayne left, she glanced in her rearview mirror. Ben remained in place, staring at her car, eyes narrowed.

Was that because of the sun or was it something else, something he wasn't telling her?

She glanced at his card.

Cummings Enterprises. Hardly a descriptive business name.

"The work on that house wasn't cheap," she mused. "Whatever he does, he surely must have funds to pay for landscaping. I could ask for a big deposit."

Ben Cummings was an enigma.

For the first time in her life Jayne was intrigued by a man. Funny how that made her heart skip a beat. Of course, it wasn't just Ben who had her worked up. There was that loan company, Restart, to consider, too—but it was silly to waste time dreaming about them. She probably wouldn't get a loan.

But if Rose's Roses didn't soon sell… Jayne couldn't consider that. Losing Grandma Em was unthinkable.

Why didn't God help?

Maybe she'd done something, offended Him somehow. Maybe that's why she never got the answers she prayed for. Maybe God was sick and tired of Jayne Rose and her constant needs.

She thought of Ben. He seemed confident at church, confident at his house, just plain confident. If only she could be like that. But fear wouldn't let go of her.

Fear that somehow, sometime, someway, she would lose everything.

Again.

Chapter Three

Three days later, Ben found himself inside Rose's Roses again.

"Hello." Jayne gave him a funny look. "I haven't quite finished your landscaping plans yet," she said, her confusion evident.

"I didn't expect you would have," he assured her. "I'm here on a different mission."

"Hello, Ben." Emma's color was better this morning. She smiled at him, though her hands never stopped their intricate braiding of a daisy chain. "A baby dedication," she explained with a tiny laugh.

"Ah. How are you?" he asked, charmed by her lovely smile.

"I'm well today."

It was the *today* that got him. How long before Restart notified Jayne about her loan and Emma got her surgery? He'd ask later.

"I'm here to talk about Easter." Ben held up a hand when Jayne opened her mouth. "I know, you told me it was too early for potted lilies. I'll come back to order them. For now I need to discuss the Easter-morning service. I understand you ladies always do the decorating."

"Yes." Emma's face saddened. "My son and his wife were killed on Easter morning. He was a horticulturalist and Jayne's mom a botanist. Jayne and I do the church's Easter flowers as our tribute to their memory."

"That's a wonderful memorial." Ben swallowed. Why hadn't anyone warned him?

"What about Easter?" Jayne said.

"The pastor asked if I'd help with the service. He said I should talk to you so we can coordinate."

"Is he planning something special?" Jayne seemed surprised.

"He wants to open the service with the Biblical scene from the garden, when Mary Magdalene and Peter arrive at the tomb. I wondered if you two could create a garden scene in front of the tomb opening."

"Of course we can." Emma pulled a pen and pad near and began sketching.

"You'd have to find someone to build the tomb part," Jayne warned.

"Of course." When Emma left to help a customer, Ben moved nearer Jayne. "Have you heard anything about your loan application yet?"

"I haven't filled it out."

"Why not?" he asked in consternation.

"I don't have a down payment, Ben. Nothing." Her stormy eyes glared at him. "They're not going to loan me money to buy Rose's Roses without a down payment."

"You don't know that." He didn't understand her hesitation. "Do you have some other plan to get Emma her surgery?"

"No." Her look told him to butt out.

"Then send in the application. The worst Restart can do is say no."

She wanted to say something, but Emma returned with a friend in tow.

"I know I'd promised to help you, dear, but would you mind if we went for lunch first? We're planning the ladies' spring retreat."

"Go." Jayne shooed her grandmother out the door. "And don't come back early," she called.

"Speaking of lunch," Ben said. "Are you free? I hate eating alone."

"What about the friend you were going to buy the flowers for?"

"Had lunch with her last week. I don't want to be a pest." He grinned. "Come on. It's my treat."

"You're sure you want to go with me?" Jayne studied him from behind the thick glasses, her turquoise eyes shadowed with doubt.

"I wouldn't ask if I didn't. Maybe we could talk more about the Easter thing."

"Yes," she said quickly. "Of course. I'll get my purse."

The way Jayne scurried away left Ben wishing he hadn't used Easter as the excuse to get her to join him. Now she'd think he'd asked her solely so they could discuss his Easter ideas, which was not his intent.

Jayne Rose was a puzzle Ben wanted to solve. He'd watched her among the flowers, totally confident, full of solutions and able to deal with evolving situations. He'd seen the sparkle in her eyes when she took stock of his yard and considered the landscaping possibilities. She *said* she wanted to buy her grandmother's business, but given a possible opportunity, she'd shied away, and Ben wanted, needed, to know why.

Jayne introduced him to Sidney, who had emerged from the back of the shop. After giving her helper some instructions, Jayne led the way to the door.

"Where's a good place to eat?" he asked as they strolled

down the sidewalk. Jayne's gait was slightly uneven as she favored her right leg. Funny, he hadn't noticed that before.

"I guess it depends on what you like to eat," she deferred. She flushed a dark red when some passersby paused to stare at them. Actually they were staring at *him,* but Jayne wouldn't know that.

"You choose."

She selected a small café tucked between two upscale boutiques.

"It's not fancy, but the food is good." She chose a table near the back.

After they'd been served, Ben realized he was going to have to initiate the conversation.

"Have you come up with any good ideas for my yard?"

"Lots of them." Immediately her demeanor changed. Her face glowed with interest. She removed her glasses, leaned forward and began to speak in a strong voice, one finger rubbing the bridge of her nose. "It could go several ways, though. I can't decide which because I don't know enough about you."

Uh-oh.

"There's not much to know," he prevaricated. "I'm a pretty boring guy."

"You own a company."

"Yes."

"What are your hobbies? Besides reading," she added.

"I swim. I'm interested in photography." He shrugged. "I used to ski but there's little chance of that here."

"You might find some snow if you go up the mountain, though you won't be able to ski," she teased. "But you could hike up, or take the aerial tramway. The view across the Coachella Valley is fantastic on a clear day."

"I might do that."

"You're not from anywhere around here, are you?"

"Why do you say that?"

"You have a kind of accent. It's different. I'm guessing Canadian?"

"Yes." Ben was surprised by her acuity. "But how did you know?"

"A lot of snowbirds winter in Palm Springs. I've learned to distinguish voices." She grinned. "If you like skiing, I'm guessing you're not here to escape the snow."

"Actually I was living in Los Angeles, but I hated the rat race. I wanted someplace near enough to do business when I have to, but with a quieter pace. Palm Springs fits."

"Do you have family?"

It was clear to Ben that he was going to have to offer some details or Jayne would simply keep probing.

"No. My mother died when I was born. My father had a heart attack when I was nine. I have no other family."

"I'm sorry." She frowned. "Nine is awfully young to be left alone. Who raised you?"

"I had a guardian. He's gone now." Relieved when their server refreshed their beverages, Ben turned the tables. "What about you?"

"I grew up in a little town called Greendale, in Colorado. My parents had a nursery business." Jayne tasted her salad.

"That's where you caught the landscaping bug?"

"Yes. My parents taught me a lot." She paused, fork midair, and smiled. "When we visited my grandmother, we'd go into the desert and I'd learn the differences between there and home."

The wistful note in her voice made Ben realize how much she'd lost.

"I'm sorry they're gone, Jayne. It must have been hard for you."

"I had Granny Em." Her voice had hardened.

"Yes, but still. You had to change schools. That's never easy for a teen."

"It was horrible." The words burst out of her. Once she'd spoken, she sipped her iced tea and stared straight ahead.

Jayne was full of stress. He could see it in the way she gripped her glass. She needed to talk to someone and probably didn't want to burden Emma.

"What was the worst part?"

"The other students," she admitted quietly, too quietly. "I missed a lot of time while I was in the hospital recovering from the accident. That put me behind everyone. The school I went to here had mostly wealthy kids with all the expensive toys kids dream of."

"And you didn't," he murmured.

"No. Emma and her partner had just started the business back then. There wasn't a lot of extra money. My parents didn't carry much insurance because their business was also new and they were struggling to build it." She squeezed her eyes closed. A moment later she murmured, "But it wasn't just the things."

Ben ate slowly, content to let her speak without breaking her train of thought.

"It was the way the kids acted. They laughed at me." Anguish threaded her soft tones. She covered it quickly. "I suppose I was funny. Suddenly I had to wear glasses to focus and I couldn't get used to them. I bumped into everything. I was a klutz. Still am sometimes."

"That wasn't your fault."

"No, but that didn't matter to them."

"Why?"

"Because I didn't fit in," she said so softly he had to lean forward to hear. "No matter what I did, I could never be one of them. I tried, but I didn't know how."

"Teenagers are horrible," he agreed in quiet understanding.

"I went to boarding schools. The only kid who didn't go home for Christmas."

"But your guardian?"

"He had to travel for his work."

"Oh." She sighed. "I was used to horseback riding and white-water rafting. The students at school were all about fashion. I couldn't afford new clothes, even if I'd known how to dress like them. In Colorado my mother made my clothes. I thought they looked great, but the kids here mocked them. They called me Country Mouse."

"It didn't help that you couldn't be on the cheerleading squad, I suppose."

"How—?" Her head jerked up. She stared at him.

"Lucky guess," Ben explained. "Your leg…you favor it. I'm guessing it was damaged in the accident." His heart wrenched at her sad nod.

"I had a lot of surgery on my knee, so no sports. And in that school, sports were king. They were state champions in almost everything. Football, basketball, volleyball. You name it."

"You didn't have any friends?"

"I did, for a while. A good friend. We were the science geeks. But in my junior year she moved away. Then I was really alone." Jayne pushed away her plate, pulled on her glasses and grimaced. "I sound pathetic."

"You sound like you suffered," he corrected.

"It's just that…I had so many dreams," she murmured. "Before the accident—oh, it doesn't matter."

"Yes, it does." Ben reached out and grasped her fingers with his. "I can understand how going through what you did has made you doubt yourself, Jayne. I understand that you feel hesitant about reaching for something that seems out of reach."

"Yes." She slid her hand from his and hid it under the table.

"But you've been a churchgoer for a long time, I think. You know about God."

"I haven't had much success in gaining His help lately," she admitted, keeping her head bent so he couldn't see into her eyes. "I've prayed so hard for an answer to help Granny Em, but nothing seems to work."

"Maybe Restart is part of God's answer." Ben tucked his forefinger under her chin and nudged it up so he could see her amazing eyes. "What have you got to lose?" he asked after a long silence.

Jayne stared at him for endless moments. Finally she balled up her napkin and set it on the table. Her anger radiated like nuclear fallout.

"What did I say?"

"You don't understand," she told him fiercely.

"I'm trying. Tell me."

"You think it's simply a matter of 'if at first you don't succeed, try again.'" A bitter edge made her musical voice sound harsh.

"It's not?"

"I have tried again," she said with a fervor that clouded her eyes. "And again. When I didn't win the scholarship to get my botany degree at the college of my choice, I tried again. But I had to have another surgery and lost my chance. Twice."

"That stinks," he agreed.

"So I decided to focus on Rose's Roses. I figured I'd expand into landscaping and prove myself there. Now even that dream is gone. I have to find a buyer for the shop so that I can pay for Emma's surgery." She sagged against her chair. "Every time I get my courage screwed up enough to try again, to believe God has something special in store for me, I take another hit."

"And after a while it's too hard to trust one more time, to

believe once again that God will hear and answer your prayers." Ben nodded. "I know. I've been there, believe me."

"Sure." She doubted him.

Ben couldn't explain without telling her the secrets he'd always kept hidden. She was in a vulnerable place. She needed money. If she knew he was wealthy—well, Ben wasn't ready to trust Jayne with that information.

As the son of a wealthy tycoon, Ben had learned early that his money got between him and people. That had become more evident since his success as bestselling author David Bentley. People envied him the things money could buy. They assumed a few bucks could solve any problem. Few understood that money couldn't buy trust or relationships where you could honestly be yourself.

"I've embarrassed you," Jayne said. "I'm sorry. It's not your fault. I guess you caught me at a low spot."

"I'm not embarrassed. I appreciate honesty. I think God does, too." Ben knew she wanted to leave from the way she kept checking the wall clock. "But you can't give up on God, Jayne. He doesn't dangle a carrot in front of you and then jerk it away when you get too close. God isn't like that."

"Uh-huh."

"God is the giver of dreams. He places dreams and ambitions and goals in our hearts because He wants us to achieve them." Her skepticism was palatable. "We don't understand His ways sometimes, but that doesn't mean He wants our failure."

"I really have to go," she said, rising.

"Okay." Ben paid the bill, walked back to the shop with her. "But will you send in the application to Restart? Please? Give God one more chance."

She paused in front of her display window, her face troubled. "Why is this so important to you?"

"Because I believe God has good things in store for you and I want you to experience them," he said. "I don't want you to regret not applying and later realize your fears might have prevented Emma from getting the surgery she needs."

"My fears?" Her brows lowered angrily.

"God can't help if you let fear control you," he offered quietly.

Jayne took a long time, but finally she nodded. "I'll think about it."

"Great!" Ben was so relieved by her answer he bent and kissed her cheek.

"I'll have your estimate ready by Friday," she said, one hand covering the spot he'd kissed. "Thanks for lunch."

Before he could answer, she disappeared inside Rose's Roses.

Ben hurried away. He wasn't sorry he'd kissed her, though he was pretty sure Jayne might be.

It was time for him to talk to God about Jayne Rose.

Long after her grandmother had retired that night, Jayne sat staring at the documents Ben had given her.

God can't help if you let fear control you.

Was that what she was doing? Was that why, when she sat in church, she didn't feel anything? Because fear was blocking out God?

Emma needed that surgery. Jayne had done everything else she could think of to make it happen. Now she had to do this.

Quickly, allowing no second thoughts, Jayne filled out the Restart paperwork then sealed everything in the envelope provided. She tucked it into her purse. Tomorrow she'd mail it, but she'd tell no one. Just in case she failed again.

Because she wasn't sleepy, Jayne pulled out her plans for Ben's landscape. Were they too grand? Too unusual? Would Ben laugh at her grandiose dreams?

Ben was nice and polite, so he probably wouldn't laugh.

But he might not give her the contract, either. Some people couldn't see her vision. Maybe he'd choose someone else.

The thought of not getting the job stopped the breath in her throat. She really, really wanted to do that yard.

Two days. She had two days before she presented her schemes.

Grabbing a pencil and a new sheet of paper, Jayne began sketching another plan. A simpler plan. A plan that said nothing about her innovative ideas. A plan that everyone would like.

Filling out a loan application was a risk she was prepared to take. But losing this job because she wanted to prove her abilities was a risk she couldn't afford.

"It isn't fear," Jayne told herself as dawn lit the sky. "It's practicality. Granny Em and I need this job."

But in her heart, the burst of excitement she'd first felt was gone.

Chapter Four

Ben shifted uncomfortably in his office chair and scrambled for a way out.

"So, what do you think?" Jayne's big green eyes studied him hopefully.

"It's not what I expected," he admitted, hating the way disappointment erased her smile.

"You don't like my design."

"I didn't say that," he muttered, avoiding her eyes.

"You didn't have to." She gathered up her drawings and stuffed them into the portfolio she'd brought. "I have to get back. Emma isn't feeling well today."

"Jayne." Ben rose, placed a hand on her arm. "I don't mean…" He stopped, at a loss for words. How did you tell someone their ideas were boring, old-school stuff and you'd expected innovative, groundbreaking, modern ideas?

"It's fine. Really. Thanks for the opportunity. I have to go." Jayne scurried out of his house and off his property as if he'd threatened her. She never noticed when one of her design sheets fluttered to the floor.

Ben picked it up, but she was gone before he could call out.

He shoved it in his pocket while watching the cloud of red-brown dust follow her van through his gates. He returned inside, made himself a cup of coffee and carried it out to his back deck. There he sat down on a rusty chair and surveyed his favorite part of the yard. The pool was the first thing he'd had repaired and cleaned. It had become his solace.

He pulled out Jayne's sketch.

Only this wasn't Jayne's work. The boring use of space around the pool didn't match the excitement on her face as she'd trailed around his grounds that Sunday afternoon. Ben could reconcile nothing about the presentation he'd just seen with the vibrant quick thinker who'd scrawled idea after idea across her notepad, blissfully lost in possibilities. This design was—he hunted for the right word—safe.

In a flash Ben knew what had happened. Jayne needed money for her grandmother's operation, therefore she needed this job. And she wasn't willing to risk losing it on atypical ideas she probably thought he'd reject. But, the thing was, Ben wanted the unusual, the unexpected. He wanted her innovations.

He'd only caught a glance at Jayne's sketches that Sunday afternoon, but Ben was almost positive she had originally planned something quite different for his yard. He'd seen from her floral work that she was inventive. Nothing at Rose's Roses looked ordinary, not the way this sketch did. This was a waste of her talents.

Ben had to find a way to get Jayne to let go of the fear and take a risk. But how?

"She's gifted, Lord. She's got vision, if she'd only let herself believe in it, in You." As he so often had in the past, Ben prayed for a way to help another whose faith needed bolstering.

Half an hour later he had an idea. Time to visit Emma.

* * *

Jayne couldn't believe what she was reading.

Your loan has been approved. A representative from Restart will contact you within the next two days to complete the paperwork and initiate the transaction.

"Granny! Granny, listen to this!"

Emma was delighted, of course, but her excitement was tempered by her weakened state. Because she'd felt too ill to leave her bed today, Jayne had used her lunch hour to run home and warm some soup for her beloved grandmother's lunch. This news made the trip across town even more worthwhile.

"I'm going to call the doctor's office and find out when we can schedule the operation."

"You don't have the money yet, dear," Granny Em's weak voice chastised.

"Aren't you the lady who's always telling me to have some faith?" Jayne chided. "Pray, Granny." If Emma asked, surely God would answer.

Jayne waited till her grandmother had whispered a short prayer for guidance before calling the doctor's office. She was stunned when the operation was set for three days later.

"What is it?" Granny Em asked.

Jayne knelt by her grandmother's bed and relayed the news as tears streamed down her cheeks.

"So why are you weeping, my dear?" The small gnarled fingers lovingly threaded through Jayne's hair in a delicate caress. "This is what we've been waiting for."

"I know." Jayne buried her face in the bedclothes. "But I'm afraid, Granny Em. Open-heart surgery…" She gulped. "It's so dangerous. I can't lose you. You're the only one I have left."

"You always have God, Jayne," Emma reminded. "I can't

be here forever, but He can. Don't you remember our reading from the Psalms this morning? 'Though a mighty army surrounds me, my heart will know no fear.' There are so many scriptures telling us not to be afraid."

"I know. But sometimes—" Jayne bit her lip. Why burden Emma when she must be having her own doubts? "I'll try to remember, Granny." She kissed the pale cheek and stood. "I guess I'd better get back to work."

"I'll read a bit more before I do those dishes."

"What are you reading?"

"A novel by David Bentley. You said Ben had a lot of them in his office. I thought I'd find out what the attraction is."

"Oh. Well, enjoy." It was futile to tell her grandmother to leave the dishes for her, so Jayne didn't bother. Half an hour later she was back at Rose's Roses, where Sidney couldn't contain her relief at the news of the loan.

"So you'll be my boss," she said and giggled. "As if you aren't already. I'm so glad for Emma. What changes will you make here, Jayne?"

"Not many. We'll keep doing what we've been doing, trying to grow the business."

"Yes." Moments later Sidney left on her own lunch break.

Jayne reworked the window display, her spirit uplifted as it hadn't been for weeks. She finished just as Sidney returned. Together they loaded the day's deliveries and Sidney left again. Between customers, Jayne updated her ledgers then reshelved the giftware section. The dream of landscaping Ben's yard repeatedly fluttered through her brain, but she shoved it away. He'd had days to decide. She knew she'd lost the contract. If only she'd risked—

Jayne blinked, startled by the sight of Ben strolling into the shop, as if she'd somehow conjured him with her frequent thoughts.

"Hi," he greeted her, his manner as friendly as usual. "Is Emma around?"

"She's at home today," Jayne told him, fiddling with a fern she'd already watered. "Can I help?"

"Nothing important. I was just going to chat. About Easter." He watched her arrange place settings on a glass table. "The cat teapot you had in the window is gone."

Ben seemed to have a fascination with window displays.

"Yes. A tourist bought it this morning." Jayne couldn't keep the news to herself any longer. "I got the loan," she said.

"Great!" A wide grin displayed his perfect teeth. Did he have to look so good all the time? "I knew you would."

"You did?" She studied him curiously. "How?"

"Well, you're so talented. I can understand why they'd want to loan you that money, because you certainly know what you're doing here. At Rose's Roses, I mean." Ben blinked, opened his mouth and then quickly closed it.

"Thank you." He was acting oddly, Jayne decided.

"Do you have time to celebrate? There's a new coffee place around the corner. They have a picture in the window of these mile-high cinnamon buns—"

Jayne started laughing.

"You and your window-shopping." She shook her head. "Thanks anyway, but I've got too much to do."

"How about dinner tonight?" Ben frowned. "Oh, you said Emma's not well. Okay, what if I brought something over? You could both relax."

"It's nice of you, but…" Jayne didn't want Emma around when Ben told her she hadn't received the contract. But she couldn't say that because a group of ladies arrived to seek her advice on table centerpieces for their annual luncheon fund-raiser.

Ben hung around for a while, but when no solution was

easily achieved with her customers, he raised a hand in fare-well and left.

"What a handsome man," Mrs. Bartle said. "I feel like I should know him."

"He just moved here," Jayne offered, wishing they'd make a decision so she could finish and maybe get home early.

"I'm sure I should know who he is."

"His name is Ben Cummings."

"Never heard that name before. I guess I was wrong." But for the rest of their time together, Mrs. Bartle kept glancing toward the door.

The women left as Sidney returned.

"You look a little frazzled, Jayne. What did those five sweet ladies do to make you look like that?" she teased.

"Only asked to see about every flower known to man. And guess what they selected for their midsummer luncheon? Daisies," she said in disgust. "I answered a thousand questions about orchids and they chose daisies." She sighed. "I'm beat."

"Why don't you go home? I'll close up here. With all those golf masters in town, everyone's pretty much on the course anyway, hoping to catch a glimpse of the rich and famous."

"You don't mind?" Relieved, Jayne left ten minutes later. She stopped by the grocery store on her way and chose a ready-made supper. She was too tired to cook.

When she opened the door to her grandmother's condo, Ben was in the kitchen, humming as he lifted lids that allowed delicious aromas to tease her nose.

"Hi," he greeted her with a grin.

"Hi, yourself. What are you doing?"

"Cooking dinner. It's a hobby of mine."

"Cooking is?" She frowned. "You never mentioned it before."

"It's a new one." He turned off a timer. "Your grandmother

is reading in her room. Dinner will be ready in ten minutes. Does that give you enough time?"

To do what? But Jayne never asked. She was too bemused by the sight of big, tall Ben wrapped in one of her grandmother's pale pink aprons, holding a darker pink pot mitt in one hand. He had a feather-brush of flour on one cheek and a stain of tomato sauce below his right eye. He looked adorable.

"Here." He lifted the grocery bags from her arms. "I'll put these away while you freshen up."

"Thanks." Jayne went to check on her grandmother. "What's going on?"

"Ben wanted to celebrate you getting the loan. He offered to make dinner and I accepted. Are you upset?" Emma asked, a worried furrow pleating her forehead.

"Of course not." She looked around. "Did you finish your book?"

"Yes. It was very insightful. Wear that pretty green sundress that brings out your eyes," Emma suggested. "You always look so lovely in it."

"It's rather fancy for dinner at home, isn't it?" Jayne gave her grandmother a speculative glance. "You're not matchmaking, are you, Granny?"

"Ben's a nice man who's making us dinner. I simply thought we could make it an occasion." Emma began primping. "Don't be too long, dear."

"No." Bemused, Jayne entered her own room and sank onto the bed. She'd lived with Emma a long time, learned to read her unspoken signals. And right now Jayne's radar told her Emma was up to something. Maybe not matchmaking, but something.

Jayne would be on her guard during this meal, for some sign that would explain Emma's unusual attitude.

But as they shared Ben's excellent cooking on Emma's balcony, Jayne was hard-pressed to identify her grandmother's motives as she asked question after question. Ben fielded most of them without giving away much.

"Are you worried I'm a wolf in sheep's clothing?" he finally teased.

"Maybe." Emma sipped her tea. "It was a lovely dinner, Ben, thank you. But I think I'll retire now. I'm quite tired." She rose, kissed Jayne's cheek, gave Ben another of her thoughtful gazes, and then left them alone together.

"I'm sorry. I don't know what's gotten into her. I'm sure she wasn't prying," Jayne apologized.

"Of course she was." Ben laughed. "She's protecting her baby. You. I can't fault her on that."

Because she didn't know how to respond, Jayne began clearing the table.

"I made this mess," Ben protested, "so I'm washing. But I'll gladly accept help drying."

"It does seem as if you've used every dish we own," Jayne mused, stunned by the mess in the kitchen.

"You have to crack a few eggs to make an omelet," he said cheerily as he began scrubbing. "That's what my new cookbook said. I saw it in—"

"The window of the bookstore," she finished, laughing.

Since Ben didn't mention his landscaping job, neither did Jayne. She knew he hadn't been thrilled with her plans. Neither was she. Maybe…

"You must be concerned about the operation," he said when they were again seated on the balcony, sipping lemon-mint iced tea. His brown eyes studied her. "But you don't have to be. Emma will be fine."

"You can't know that."

"I *believe* that," he said. He reached out and covered her fingers with his, holding them for just a moment, then squeezing and letting go. "I trust God."

"You make it sound so easy." That sniggle of fear in her stomach winched a fraction tighter.

"It gets easier the more you do it, Jayne." His beautiful smile blazed. "But you have to start, take a stand, insist to your doubting brain that God is who He says He is, that He always keeps His word."

"How do I do that?" she asked, embarrassed that she had to ask after all these many years of calling herself a Christian.

"Whenever the doubts start creeping in, you push them back with a Scripture verse. 'When I am afraid, I will put my confidence in You. I will trust the promises of God.' Or, 'Oh God, my strength! I will sing Your praises, for You are my place of safety.'" He leaned forward, his face inches from hers. "After you've repeated them long enough, your head will accept what your mouth is saying and the fear will lose its power."

She vaguely remembered the same advice from high school days when she'd briefly joined a youth group. She'd let bad memories of her high school troubles crowd out the group leader's teaching. She should have been stronger.

"I have one favorite verse I repeat to myself when things get really bad. Want to hear it?"

"Yes." Since Ben was strong and confident, Jayne was willing to emulate what was clearly successful.

"It's from the sixtieth Psalm when King David reminded himself that he wasn't alone. He said, 'God has promised to help us. He has vowed it by His holiness!' Those are strong words. A powerful promise, one you can depend on, Jayne."

"Thank you." The usual awkwardness rushed in. Jayne kept her head bent.

"The day of Emma's operation," Ben said softly. "Do you mind if I'm there? Maybe there's something I could do, or—"

"You don't need a reason," Jayne told him, squeezing all her courage together to meet his gaze. "We'd love to have you there. Emma has to go in tomorrow night for prep." She swallowed past the lump in her throat. "She has a lot of friends and they'll be praying." *But I could use a friend, too.*

"Then I'll pick you up the next morning and we'll see her before she goes in. Okay?"

"Thank you," Jayne said, and meant it.

"It's getting late. I'd better go."

Jayne walked Ben to the door. When he paused before opening it, she rushed into speech to prevent an awkward moment.

"I appreciate the dinner. And the advice," she murmured. "So does Emma."

"Friends help friends," he said quietly. Then he bent and brushed her cheek with his lips. "Good night, friend."

He was gone before she could say a word.

Jayne closed the door and leaned against it, her mind fluttering from one bit of conversation to another, but always returning to that kiss. She wasn't a romantic kind of person, but Ben made her think about possibilities.

After a moment, Jayne shook herself free of the fantasies and returned to the patio, this time with her Bible. She paged through it until she found the verses Ben quoted. She underlined and highlighted each one, even copied two on small notepaper that she taped to her bedroom mirror. And then she found a verse of her own.

My protection and success come from God alone.

Jayne repeated the words until a gentle whisper of peace crept into her heart and nestled there. If only she could find that same peace whenever she thought about her grandmother's surgery.

At least Ben would be there with her.

Chapter Five

"Come back to me, Granny," Jayne whispered. She kissed her grandmother's cheek, stepped back and let go of the frail white fingers. She watched, heart in her mouth, as the nurses wheeled away the only family she had left.

"Emma's in God's hands now." Ben wrapped a comforting arm around her shoulders and steered her to the waiting room. When Jayne was seated, he handed her a small book.

"Window-shopping, again?" she asked, struggling to smile.

"I thought it might be of some help to you."

The way he said it made Jayne glance at the cover. *Questions about God.*

"I don't know if I can concentrate on this today," she said. "Maybe you should have brought me one of your David Bentley books. Emma was reading one the other day."

"Oh." Ben shuffled through the available magazines, his face averted from her. "Did she like it?"

"She said it was enlightening." Jayne waited until he was seated. "You obviously like him," she said. "You have enough of his books."

"I'm kind of a book collector." He began reading as if to indicate that he didn't want to talk.

Jayne flipped open the cover of her book and pretended to peruse it, but the truth was, she was too nervous to concentrate. A flock of butterflies performed a nervous dance inside her stomach, making it impossible to even sip the coffee Ben brought. And it didn't seem to matter how often she repeated the verses she'd memorized; doubts pushed their way into her brain. She watched the minutes tick past on the big silver clock and felt a cloak of worry enshroud her.

"What's taking so long?" she fussed. Two hours had passed and she could no longer stay seated. Or think about anything but Emma and how much she loved her.

"The doctor said three hours minimum." Ben's fingers threaded through hers. "Let's go for a little walk around the grounds."

"But if something happens, I want to be here."

"Jayne." He shook his head. "Have some faith."

The atmosphere stifled her. She needed fresh air to breathe, but—

"Come on. We'll tell the nurses where we're headed."

She capitulated because she needed to get out of there, needed to walk off some of her pent-up energy. Ben kept hold of her hand as they followed the pathways between stunning beds of flowers blooming brightly in the warm sun. Emma would love—

"'I am like a sheltered olive tree protected by the Lord Himself. I trust in the mercy of the Lord forever and ever,'" Ben said in a voice meant for her ears alone. "'God is my helper. He is a friend of mine.'"

On and on, Ben's continual recitations of the Psalms flowed like a warm healing salve over her spirit. And as they walked, the words began to soak into her soul until Jayne was able to repeat the words with him.

"Better now?" he asked when they paused in front of the main hospital doors.

"Yes. Much. Thank you." She studied the firm strength in his face, the honest clarity of his eyes. "I mean it. Thank you so much."

"You just needed a reminder of God's goodness. It's easy to let ourselves get ground down by fear and worry, but that's exactly when we need to trust in God's goodness." He squeezed her fingers tightly then let them go. "King David said it best. 'This one thing I know; God is for me.' You can't let go of that promise, Jayne. You can't let yourself begin to doubt His goodness or you'll find that doubt takes over your mind."

"I'll try," she promised as they rode the elevator.

But by the time Emma's doctor appeared, Jayne's confidence was wobbling.

"Emma's come through the surgery very well. She's in recovery now. She'll be back in her room in a little while. You can see her for a few moments, but then she must rest."

Jayne thanked him, made a quick call to give Sidney the good news, then grabbed Ben's hand and led him to Emma's room. When she realized what she'd done, she flushed hotly and dropped his hand. Ben laughed as he hugged her for a few precious seconds.

"I told you that you could trust God," he said.

"Yes, you did." Again the questions about his past life, how he'd become the man he was, flooded her mind. He'd probably bow out of their lives after this. When would she get a better opportunity to learn more about him? "How did you come to have such strong faith, Ben?" she asked.

"I had a teacher in high school. Mr. Gabriel." Ben's big brown eyes softened like chocolate melting in the desert. "He taught me my love of literature and he lived showing God's love. He's gone now but his lessons have never left me."

"I wish I'd had someone like him in high school. How many years did he teach you?"

"Three. Listen, can I get you a drink or something to eat? You must be starving. It's well past lunchtime."

"No, thanks." She wanted to know more. "What happened during summer? You didn't have to stay at the boarding school, did you?"

"No. I usually went to summer camp." He rattled the change in his pocket. "Are you sure you can't eat—"

"Not till Granny Em comes back." She pushed on, curiosity roused. "Summer camp's expensive, isn't it? Some of the kids in our school used to go, some of the richest ones. Their parents were usually in Europe or something."

"Oh."

Frustrated by his lack of response, Jayne kept probing. "Did you like camp?"

"I liked the swimming."

"Was it at a lake?" Why did she feel as though she was pulling hen's teeth to get him to talk?

"Sometimes. Other years it was just a camp."

"In Canada, I suppose?" Jayne watched his face close up and knew she'd pushed too hard.

"Umm," was all he said. Relief flooded his eyes as a commotion in the hall announced Emma's arrival.

The nurses wheeled her in and made her comfortable. They said the doctor had approved a ten-minute visit, but no longer.

Jayne stared at the washed-out face and the myriad of tubes running from her grandmother's tiny body. For a second, doubts assailed her. Why didn't God—

"Remember, Jayne. God is here for her."

"Yes." Jayne kissed Emma's cheek, enfolded the tiny hand in her own and felt Emma's pulse beating sure and strong. Her grandmother's eyelids fluttered open for a minute and she smiled then drifted off to sleep. "I'll be back later, Granny," she promised. "I love you."

Then with the nurse watching, Jayne left the room, suddenly weary beyond words.

"Let's have lunch now. Then you need to go home and rest."

"Rest?" She stepped into his vehicle and bumped her arm against the door, which made her glad she didn't have to drive. "I have work to do."

"Not today, Jayne." He climbed in on his own side and started the engine. "You were up this morning at five, I'm guessing. And you probably didn't sleep much last night. You need to take care of yourself so you're strong and ready to help Emma when she comes home. So lunch, then rest, right?"

"I guess you're the boss. For now," she warned, trying to infuse some spunk into her voice.

Ben took her to a lovely place where the fragrance of fresh-baked bread filled the room. After a delicious meal he insisted they share a slice of strawberry pie.

"It's very fresh."

Jayne tasted and agreed. "Do you eat here a lot?"

"Not a lot. But some. My cooking repertoire extends to what I cooked for you and Emma, baked beans and a take-out menu," he admitted. "I do make a mean piece of toast, though."

"Funny, I thought a guy on his own would have learned to fend for himself," she murmured, sipping the last of her iced tea.

For a moment he just stared at her. Long seconds passed, making Jayne think she'd said something wrong. Finally he laughed, but it was forced and unnatural.

"I do fend," he said jauntily. "Toast with peanut butter. Toast with jam. Toast by itself."

"A veritable chef," she agreed. She couldn't ignore his odd manner but it went out of her mind when he drove up in front of her building and walked her to the door.

"Lie down for a while, okay? Today's been tough on you." He brushed her cheek with his knuckles. "But don't forget what I said. God cares. He is good."

"I'll try." She couldn't possibly tell him how much his presence with her had meant. "I suppose you've lost a lot of time working today," she began and stopped when her neighbor Barney appeared and stared at Ben.

"Hey, aren't you—"

"No, I'm not. Sorry." Ben ignored Barney's blink of surprise. "Bye." He smiled at Jayne once more then walked away.

"Do you know that guy, Jayne?"

"Of course. His name is Ben Cummings. He's a friend of Emma's and mine."

"Oh. I thought he was someone else." All the way up in the elevator Barney peppered her with questions about Emma. "You tell me when she's home," he said as they walked to their doors. "I'll bring her some of my chicken soup."

"I'll do that," Jayne promised. Inside the apartment, the rooms seemed empty without Emma. "But she's coming home," she told herself. "That's the main thing."

As she lay on the chaise on the balcony, waiting for sleep to claim her, Jayne suddenly remembered the odd encounter earlier and wondered who Barney had thought Ben was. She'd have to ask him sometime.

"Yes, Pastor, Ben did tell us about plans for the Easter-morning service. I'd be pleased to be on the planning committee." Jayne snuggled the shop's portable telephone between her ear and her shoulder as she fiddled with a floral order marked urgent. "By the way, thank you for visiting Emma. I know she enjoyed it."

"I'm delighted she's doing so well. You're both an important part of our congregation. And we always appreciate the work you do to make our Easter services so special."

"We'll be happy to help with whatever you need." Jayne promised to attend the first planning meeting. After he'd hung up, she needed lunch. "I'll just grab a sandwich and come back. Maybe then I can get caught up on these convention flowers."

"I don't think so," Sidney said, a big grin lighting her face.

"What—?" Jayne twisted, saw Ben coming through the door. "Oh." She blushed for no reason at all.

"Hello there, beautiful ladies. Gorgeous day, isn't it?"

Certain he hadn't shown up to discuss the weather, Jayne glanced at Sidney for an answer, but Sidney was staring at Ben with something like hero worship.

"I was wondering if you'd like to share a picnic lunch with me, Jayne." He held up a wicker basket. "We could eat in the square across the street. The grass looks comfy."

"Um, I was going to grab something."

"Now you don't have to. Come on," he wheedled in that soft tone that made Jayne's heart go bump. His brown eyes twinkled. "It'll be fun."

Lunch with a handsome man? She wasn't going to say no.

Five minutes later Jayne was seated on a little red rag rug, staring at a picnic cloth loaded with delicious food.

"What's in there?" she asked, staring at a small knapsack he kept tucked behind him.

"We're going to talk about that," Ben told her. "After we eat." He gave thanks then dished out a plate for her. Neither of them had much to say as they enjoyed the meal.

"That was a lovely treat," Jayne told him when she'd eaten enough. "Thank you for such a lovely lunch."

"I had an ulterior motive." Ben took her dishes and stored them and the leftovers inside the basket. When everything was put away, he pulled forward the pack and drew out some papers.

"Those are my designs," Jayne sputtered. She looked from the papers to him, waiting for his explanation.

"Please don't be angry," he began. "But I knew those designs you showed me the other day weren't your first idea."

"You did?" She frowned.

"Yes. You got cold feet, didn't you? You thought I'd be upset if you showed me these, so you went back to the tried-and-true things that most people want in their landscapes."

"So you got Sidney to dig these out behind my back?" That peculiar smile on her employee's face suddenly made sense.

"I begged her," he admitted. "She's very loyal to you, Jayne, and she wants you to succeed. I think she finally realized that you were only hurting yourself by not showing me these."

"Hurting myself?" She couldn't absorb it. Ben was supposed to be her friend. Yet he'd coerced Sidney, made Jayne look stupid and silly in front of her own employee. It was as if she was at her high school graduation, could still feel the press of that hand on her shoulder, the sensation of falling and the horrible, mortifying snickers as everyone laughed at her. Fury raged.

"How dare you, Ben? These," she said, picking up the papers, "are not your property. They're mine. You could have asked to see them. You could have talked to me."

"I didn't think you'd show me," he said, studying her. "You were so upset after your presentation. Would you have taken the risk and shown me your ideas a second time?" His eyes bored into her.

"That's not the point." Bitterness welled up. "You said we were friends. Friends don't do this to each other."

"Friends don't try to help and encourage each other to strive for their best?" He shook his head. "What kind of friends do you have?"

"The kind who don't try to trick me," she snapped, her

pride still smarting. "I've had the kind of friend I couldn't trust, Ben. I don't want to go there again."

"If you'd just listen—"

"Why? How can I believe anything you say anymore?" She let out the pent-up frustration building inside her. "I don't really know you, Ben. And obviously you don't want me to know you."

"What?" His eyes widened. "Where did that come from?"

"From you, from the way you dance around every personal question you're asked. What are you hiding?" She'd finally said the words that had chased round her head ever since she'd met him. Jayne shoved her glasses up on her nose, wishing she didn't need the tiresome lenses to read his expression.

Right now she thought she saw fear lurking in those dark depths. But that was silly, wasn't it? Ben was never afraid.

"It's not about me." He glared at her. "I'm simply trying to help you."

"Why me?" Jayne quashed down her fears. It was better to know the truth. "Because you can't get anyone else?"

"Can't I?" His voice went deadly calm, his face became inscrutable. "I have four other landscaping bids, Jayne. They're good bids. Not too pricey. Smart designs from experienced people. Any one of them could landscape my yard."

"And you've chosen one of them, is that it? You want to tell me I lost the contract because my designs weren't as good as theirs." She shrugged, pretending it didn't hurt. "Fine. Consider me told. Now I need to get back to work." She jumped to her feet.

"I want to hire *you,* Jayne."

"What?" She froze, wrinkling her nose so her glasses would move into place and give her a clearer view of his face. "Why, when you have four others?"

"Because none of them came up with this." Ben rose, held out her sketch. "I watched you that day you came to my house. I saw some of the things you drew. Most of them weren't included in your presentation. The fountain, for instance, or that cactus area with the odd stone formations and grasses. Or the little adobe walls and the fantastic area around the pool."

She didn't know what to say so she kept silent.

"I want you to create these plans in my yard, Jayne. As soon as possible, please."

She frowned at him, anger waltzing with hope.

"You're innovative and unique. You don't do the expected, but everything I asked for is in these plans. That's why I want to hire you." Ben handed her the sheaf of designs then he slung the picnic basket over one arm.

"You need time to think it over, to make sure your estimates are right. I realize that." He folded the rug and added it to his basket. "Let me know as soon as you can start. Oh, and here's a deposit." He pulled a check out of his pocket and handed it to her. "See you," he said, then he loped across the grass.

"See you. Uh, thanks." Bemused and bewildered, Jayne stood in the sun, peering after him while her brain assimilated the information.

Her first landscaping project. She was going to get her dream!

She scrutinized the check. The amount was more than she'd asked for as a deposit.

God had answered her prayer, proof that she needed to have more faith in His love.

But as delight filled her soul, Jayne walked back to Rose's Roses with a tiny thistle of doubt wiggling its way to her brain. Though she'd challenged him, Ben hadn't told her anything new about himself. She knew no more about Ben Cummings than she had yesterday or last week.

Except that he had hired her for her first job as a landscaper and paid the deposit.

"It's up to me now, isn't it, God? With Your help I can do it."

Was learning to trust again really as simple as this?

Chapter Six

"Why is it we need to take a trip into the Mojave Desert on what must be the hottest day of the year?"

"If you think this will be the hottest day of the year, I feel sorry for you. Come July, this will feel balmy," Jayne scoffed. "And after the fuss you've created the past two weeks, pipe down and watch."

Ben grumbled under his breath. A jaunt to the desert was fine. But why must they go in her van? Uncomfortable didn't begin to describe the ride.

"Have you ever had the suspension in this thing checked?"

"The flowers have never complained." She kept both hands on the steering wheel, facing forward, her profile stern, as if she were leading a troop of soldiers.

"The bouquets probably die as soon as you deliver them." She gave him a look meant to quash. Ben sighed. "I suppose you're mad because I said that boulder is too small."

Jayne said nothing, but her mouth pursed a little tighter.

"Is the air-conditioning working in here?"

Ben turned the vent to blow full force on his face. He almost laughed when Jayne puffed to lift her bangs off her perspiring forehead. She was just as hot as he. He frowned when she did that thing with her nose to move her glasses up.

"Why don't you have the operation on your eyes?" he asked.

"Ben," she warned in an icy tone, "today is not a good day to push me."

"But—"

"You're so free with advice for everyone else," she snapped. "'Face your fears and apply for the loan, Jayne.'"

"Well, you have to admit that worked out," he said, feeling smug.

"'The rocks are too big, Jayne'" she continued in the same snappish tone. "'The wall isn't high enough, Jayne. The bushes aren't close enough to the house, Jayne.'"

"I'm only trying to help."

"Please, stop helping me. It's very frustrating." She changed lanes and once they gained the open road, she hit the gas pedal. "I'm doing my very best to create exactly what I promised, Ben. But over the past week you have questioned every single thing I've done in your yard. Even the men I've hired, patient as they are, are getting frustrated."

"You're saying I'm slowing things down?"

"Slowing? Puhleeze!" She let her gorgeous eyes do the talking, though Ben felt the awful lenses muted their scorn. "We're getting nothing done. I'm away from the shop way too much because you won't let the men follow my plans."

"I want everything perfect."

She snorted.

"Perfection doesn't exist in this world. But I can promise amazing, if you'll back off."

"So we're going into the desert because—"

"Because you've pestered me nonstop for three days about the sculptures I intend to use. So I'll show you and then you'll drop the subject. Won't you?" Her nose wiggled again. Up went the glasses.

"Yes."

"It's a long drive so sit back and enjoy the scenery. At least the desert's in bloom."

"It's beautiful."

Ben fell silent, not because he didn't have anything to say, but because he needed time to think of a way to convince Jayne to have that eye surgery. Her glasses were always teetering precariously on the end of her nose, forcing her to peer through them. She'd push them up with a dusty hand and then she couldn't see clearly through the smudges. Twice she'd lost the ugly things at a crucial moment until finally, as the desert heat grew more intense each day, she'd fastened a rubber band around her head to hold them on her sweaty nose.

Ben had pressed Emma for details about the surgery because Jayne refused to talk about it. Emma said that was because of the risk.

"Jayne's afraid she'll lose her sight."

"Would she?"

"The doctors say that if it fails, she'll likely be no worse off than she is now."

If only Ben could encourage Jayne to have a little more faith. God had given her an option. Why didn't she take it?

After an hour they stopped at a roadside stand for some cold lemonade. Ben stretched his protesting body and debated asking how much farther they had to go. Back in the van, Jayne took one hand off the wheel to hold out a bag.

"Take one. They're fresh. Best doughnuts you'll ever taste."

Ben agreed. After passing hordes of yellow blooms bursting with color against the shimmering tan-brown desert hills, he took more notice of the land and found he could distinguish some variations of cactus.

"We're here," Jayne announced half an hour later. She jumped out of the van and marched around a small adobe building.

Ben followed. And stopped short. His jaw dropped as he gaped.

"These are the kind of sculptures I want to use in your front yard," Jayne said, then greeted the small tanned woman who emerged from the building. "This is Cass Walker, the artist."

"Hello. Go ahead and look around." Cass studied him with an odd look that usually meant he'd been recognized.

Ben turned away to study her work and found himself astounded. Most were in copper or stainless, but Cass had also forged a few wrought-iron sculptures. Her creations were novel, innovative and open to interpretation. Ben had difficulty choosing a favorite.

"You'd better come out of the sun now." Jayne touched his shoulder a while later, her voice soft with a ruffle of amusement. "Cass has some iced tea for us."

Ben joined them in the shade by the building and sipped his tea, marveling that the brush of Jayne's hand on his shoulder had such an effect on his breathing. Gradually he was drawn into the two women's conversation.

They spoke as colleagues, not close friends, but there was respect in their voices. As he listened, Ben recognized Jayne's technique of drawing the other person out. She didn't give away much personal information, but spoke voluminously of her current job in Ben's yard.

"So I brought Ben to reassure him that whatever you do for us will be wonderful."

Cass smiled then asked, "How is Emma?"

"She's doing remarkably well now." Jayne explained about the surgery.

"And what do you do, Ben?"

"I manage assets." The usual noncommittal response was getting old.

"What exactly does that entail?" Cass's eyes bored into his.

"A lot of dull financial stuff," he said with a laugh and scrounged for a change of subject. "Which of these is for my place?"

"That's a surprise," Jayne interrupted. "And we have to go. Thank you so much for the tea, Cass. I hope we didn't disturb you too much."

"Not a problem." Cass studied him. "Do you have a card, Ben? You never know when I might need some financial advice."

"Sure." He pulled a card from his wallet.

"Cummings Enterprises, huh?"

"That's me," he said, recognizing her curiosity. He had a hunch she'd research him. Let her. He'd used his master's degree in finance and his lawyer, Jerry, to bury his corporation in a tangle that would take ages to unravel.

"Thanks, Cass." Jayne grinned at her. "I'll give you a call when we're ready."

She nodded but remained standing in the hot sun, watching as they drove away.

"Satisfied?" Jayne asked.

"I'm sure whatever she does will look amazing." Ben pretended nonchalance, but inside, his radar was on high alert. Cass Walker. The name was familiar and he didn't know why. And that bothered him.

He liked his privacy. He liked being known only as Ben Cummings. He liked it that most people looked at him as a regular guy and not a bank.

And he wanted to keep it that way.

Tonight he'd give Jerry a call and find out if he knew Cass Walker. Better safe than sorry.

* * *

"I'm glad you called, Cass, though I'm sorry I couldn't tell you more about Ben. I haven't known him long. Why do you want to know anyway?"

"Just curious," Cass answered.

"Well, now you know as much as I do." Jayne glanced at the clock. She was late! "I'm going to need a picture of what you've done and some dimensions so I can prepare the ground." Jayne agreed a fax would work and hung up to wait for it.

A few minutes later, fax in hand, she was ready to go back to the work site. Sidney's voice stopped her.

"Jayne, can we talk for a minute?"

"Sure. What's up?"

It took a bit of prodding, but Sidney finally admitted she was worried about business.

"We haven't been getting a lot of traffic lately. Did you see the totals for last week? We're way down over last year."

"I know." Jayne sighed. "I've been trying to work up proposals for the convention circuit in my spare time, but there's so little of that."

"You missed that Chamber of Commerce meeting yesterday because you were at Ben's. Getting publicity from them would be a real boost to our bottom line." Sidney flipped a pencil. "Would it be wrong if I contacted them and asked if we could make a last-minute proposal?"

"Can you get one together today? That first loan payment to Restart is coming up soon. A new contract would be nice."

Sidney agreed to try. Jayne's worries deepened as she drove to Ben's. If God truly had assisted in her getting the business, why would He allow it to falter?

Ben would say she had to have faith.

Jayne liked Ben, really liked him, despite his interference. Sometimes, if she worked late at the site, he'd bring her out a cold drink and insist she rest for a bit. She'd even gone swimming with him once. Those were the best times, special moments when they really clicked. But she'd begun to realize that Ben never shared much personal information. She'd garnered a tidbit here, a morsel there, but as she'd answered Cass's questions, Jayne recognized how little she actually knew about this man who was quickly becoming more than a friend.

She pulled into Ben's yard and groaned. He was talking to her men again, men that were being paid but not working. Jayne climbed out of the van and sauntered over.

"What's the problem, Glen?"

"Mr. Cummings thinks there should be more space between the wall and the seating area."

"I'll talk to Mr. Cummings. You go back to work." Ben would have interrupted but she sent him a glare. "Thank you, Glen. And next time there's a question, keep working until I say otherwise. Okay?"

"Yes, ma'am." Glen trotted away, happy to be free of the conflict. He was a good worker, fastidious about his job. He hid it better, but he was getting as frustrated as she.

"Okay, Ben, I've tried to be reasonable, but your constant interference is costing me a lot of money, money I didn't budget for." Jayne took a deep breath. "If you continue to stop work, I'm going to have to charge you for time lost. Agreed?"

"But—"

"No buts." She tried another tack. "You are constantly telling me I need to have faith. The same goes for you. Have a little faith in my ability to do as I said, will you? Otherwise, I'm going to walk away from this job."

"What? You can't," he stormed.

"I can. And I will." She grabbed his arm and drew him into the foyer of the house, where her workers couldn't overhear. "You bought my ideas, Ben. Now let me work them. I'm spending a lot of time arbitrating here. Time I'm not spending at work."

"So?" He sounded impatient.

"I have a very large loan. A loan I do not intend to default on. So if I have to put this job on hold to dig in at Rose's Roses, I will. I won't want to, but I will."

"What's wrong at Rose's Roses?"

"Sales are a pretty slow right now."

"Everyone has slow periods. How could your being there change that?"

"I wouldn't have to pay my part-time employee full-time wages, for one thing," she said quietly. "Can't you see the progress we've made here? Can't you accept that I will do as we agreed?"

"I don't know." The brown eyes held shadows of reservation.

Jayne's glasses slipped down her nose. She took them off, which made him a blur, but that was okay because what she had to say was better said without seeing his expression.

"It's not that easy for me. I want to make sure—"

"I know you're proud of this house. I know you want to make it as private as possible. I'm new, this is my first job and you don't have anything but my word to go on."

"I trust you."

"Do you? You say you trust me, but your actions say otherwise. But you are going to have to back off and let me do my job. Or I'm walking. Period. Okay?"

It took a long time for the word to slip through his lips.

"Okay."

Jayne heaved a sigh of relief.

"Thank you. Oh, by the way, Cass and I were talking today. She was asking about you."

"Was she?"

The way he said it made Jayne put her glasses back on so

she could get a good look at him. He slid on his sunglasses to shield his eyes, but not before she saw fear.

What did Ben have to be afraid of?

"Jerry? It's Ben."

"Hey! Good to hear from you."

"Same." Ben exchanged pleasantries with his lawyer for a few minutes then got to the point. "There's a woman—Cass Walker. She's an artist. Does sculptures. Do you know her?"

"Cass Walker? Yeah, sure. We went to a showing of hers about four years ago. Redondo Beach. Don't you remember?"

"No." Ben squeezed his eyes closed, trying to remember. He came up blank.

"That was the weekend your third novel with Marv Ziglar came out. Your fans were crazy for stories about that private detective." Jerry chuckled and lowered his voice to a mysterious warble. "'Who is Marv Ziglar?' Remember how everyone kept asking about that character? The publicity they stirred up made the media jump on board. You can't buy publicity like that. Everybody was talking about David Bentley. It's a wonder we managed to keep your identity a secret with all the hype that was going on."

Like a video, images played through Ben's mind. Yes, he remembered. That was the weekend he'd found out his biggest attraction to his longtime childhood friend was his money. That was the weekend he'd decided he needed to change his life. He'd resisted Jerry and his publisher's request for media interviews and book signings, and decided to get some normality back into his life. Because he'd lost a lot of weight, his look had changed. He refused a new publicity shot, hoping no one would associate the new Ben with the face on the back of his books. The publishers weren't happy, but Ben was insistent that his pseudonym was the only public face he'd put on his writing. Because David Bentley was repeatedly on the bestseller lists, they continued to publish him. Only Jerry and Ben's editor knew that David Bentley and Ben Cummings were the same man.

But Ben's clearest remembrance of that weekend was the prayer request he'd set before God, a request for a woman who would love him for who he was, and not for the money that surrounded him. A woman he could marry. Ben had been in love a couple of times, but on both occasions he'd found out that his money was his biggest attraction.

"Did you fall asleep?"

"Sorry." Ben jerked back to reality and Jerry's voice. "I think Cass recognized me. Jayne introduced me as Ben Cummings. Cass has been asking Jayne questions."

"Well I've got worse news." The vitality in Jerry's voice died. "I got your new contract last week and ever since I've been fielding calls about David Bentley's identity. I think somebody in my office is on a reporter's take. Maybe you should move again."

"No." Ben clenched his teeth. "How could this happen?"

"Money. Some people will do anything for money. You should know that." A grimness edged Jerry's voice. "Don't worry. I've taken several precautions. And when I find the leak, I'll deal with it. My staff has signed privacy agreements."

"That won't matter if they talk to some tabloid reporter. You've got to nip this before everything blows apart, Jerry."

"Already working on it. You just keep a low profile."

"As usual." Ben hung up feeling like a caged tiger.

Maybe he should give up his writing career. Ben certainly didn't need the money, although it did a lot of good for several charities. Writing also did him good. It was the one outlet where he felt totally free to express his faith. The public didn't seem to mind that Marv Ziglar, his fictional P.I., had strong moral standards, believed in God and wouldn't give up on his troubled marriage. If fact, fans wrote letters of admiration for his character.

"It's the one ministry I have," Ben murmured, talking to God as if He was right there. "You gave it to me. Am I supposed to give it up now?"

Finding no answers, Ben did what he always did when a problem knotted up his mind. He pulled on his swimming trunks and hit the pool.

But no matter how many laps he swam, a little voice in the back of his mind would not be silenced.

You tell Jayne to trust. You push her to face her fears. But though you push her for her secrets, you don't trust her with yours. Can she trust you?

Ben wasn't playing fair, and he knew it. But he couldn't forget about the past, couldn't forget he'd once made a colossal mistake by mistaking greed for love. He couldn't forget that he'd almost proposed to a woman who only saw dollar signs when she looked at him.

He wasn't going to make that mistake again, even if he had to keep his secrets a little longer.

Ben pulled himself up on the deck of the pool and stared into the night sky while he poured out his heart to the only One he could trust.

"I'm counting on You to send me the woman of Your choice, Lord. And I'm wondering. Is that woman Jayne Rose?"

Chapter Seven

"Where's Jayne? She hasn't shown up for the past three days."

Jayne recognized Ben's voice. She almost groaned, but that would have defeated her whole purpose of hiding in the back office at Rose's Roses, pretending she was working out a bid for flowers for an award presentation while she nursed her wounds.

"She'll be back at your place tomorrow," Sidney said. "No need to worry."

"But she missed our Easter meeting last night. That's the second time. Something's wrong, isn't it?" Concern laced his voice. "Is it Emma?"

"Emma's fine."

"Then what's wrong?"

"Jayne will be back at your site tomorrow."

"Where is she? You might as well tell me, Sidney, because I'm not leaving until I know what's going on."

Bother the man! Jayne rose, limped out from her hiding place.

"Is there something you need, Ben? I'm tied up here today."

"*Tied* being the operative word," he said, his lips thinning as he saw her arm in the sling. His glower grew. "What happened to your glasses?"

"A small accident." Jayne fingered the rims, knowing the big wad of adhesive tape must look ridiculous. The set of Ben's chin told her he wouldn't give up without more information. "I wasn't paying enough attention."

"Because your glasses were dirty."

"No. Well, partly," she admitted. "I was carrying some roses and didn't pay attention to where I was going."

His steady scrutiny bothered her.

"I tripped over an auger and fell into a hole." Admitting her clumsiness was embarrassing.

"So you hurt your leg, too." Ben's eyes softened sympathetically as he slid his finger along her jaw, tenderly tracing the black-and-blue bruising. "Oh, Jayne, why won't you have that operation on yours eyes and make your life simpler?"

"There's no guarantee it would do that," she muttered, easing away from his touch. Not that she didn't like him touching her, because she did. But it made her stomach feel all bubbly and effervescent. She'd never felt like that before and it was scary.

"Life doesn't come with guarantees," he said softly. "Once in a while you have to take a risk and trust God to work it out."

"Is that what you do?" She studied him.

"I try."

She pulled some yellowish leaves off a plant.

"Those flowers smell lovely," he said.

"Gardenias usually do." Jayne studied him. "Cass says she met you somewhere before. Any idea how and where you two would have crossed paths?"

"I was living in Los Angeles. I could have met her anywhere."

"Right." Jayne wasn't sure why, but she felt Ben was holding something back. "So what do you need? I'm a little busy."

"Doing what?"

"I told you Rose's Roses needs more income. I'm working on some new bids." A group of customers walked through the door. As Sidney hurried forward to help them, Jayne grabbed Ben's arm and tugged. "We can talk in the back," she murmured.

"Your leg." He waited until she'd sunk into her office chair. "You said your knee was bad. Did you pull a muscle?"

"Sort of." She sighed. "I'm fine, Ben. But I don't have time to chat. I gave the crew today off because of a funeral. They'll be back to work tomorrow, if that's what is bothering you."

"My yard can wait." He glared at her as if she'd offended him. "I was worried about you," he said, his voice sharp.

"That's nice, but as you see, I'm fine."

"Jayne, you are so not *fine*." His big brown eyes softened. "Your face is bruised. Your arm is in a sling. You're limping. You've hurt yourself so much you can't go to work."

"I *am* at work. I don't need to be at your site all the time. The crew knows what to do. Besides, we're almost finished and I have to get these bids ready. I don't have another landscaping job lined up. Rose's Roses is what keeps bread on our table, and I've got to find more income to keep it solvent. So if you don't mind…?"

Ben just stood there, watching her.

Jayne lifted her hand to nudge her glasses higher, but inadvertently touched the wrong spot. The frames fell apart and landed on her desk. For a moment she couldn't feel the lenses on her desktop and panicked.

"Don't fuss." Ben's fingers brushed against her temples as he replaced the glasses on her nose, minus the broken arm. His fingers burned against her cheek as he pushed her hair back. "Do you have another pair?" he asked gently, his breath brushing against her ear.

"I broke them last week when I tripped," she muttered, totally embarrassed. "I ordered a new pair."

"The operation could make them unnecessary. But you won't have it because you're afraid."

"You have no idea how I feel, Ben." Jayne slapped her pen on the desk and glared at him. "Do you know how many surgeries I've had since the accident? Five. Can you imagine how hard it was to push myself through the physiotherapy, the pain and the fears, to make myself keep going each time?"

"No," he admitted.

"Well, I remember it too well. So lay off."

"Dear Jayne." He rested one hip on the edge of the desk and used his fingers to force her chin up. "The point is you did it. You overcame. You succeeded. And you can do it again."

"The point is," she said sweetly, glaring at him. "I don't want to."

"Because you're afraid. Because you're not sure of God, because you don't trust Him." He cupped her cheek in his palm and leaned so close his minted breath caressed her. "You're letting fear win, Jayne, because you won't risk success."

"I'm working nonstop to be successful!"

"You're doing that to avoid thinking about the surgery." He leaned forward, brushed his lips against hers for a nanosecond, but it was enough to send her heart into overdrive. "If Rose's Roses fails, you can blame your eyes, say that your eyesight wouldn't allow you to make the changes you wanted to, or that because of the accident you didn't have the chances you needed, chances someone else would have. It's an out. But what if you didn't have that excuse?"

With a caress of his fingertips against her hair, Ben smiled and left.

Jayne sat stunned by both his words and his touch. The hum of voices from the shop barely penetrated the flurry of emotions that raced through her.

Ben was a friend, that's all. So why did she want to bury her face in his shoulder and beg him to hold her and never let go?

Because she was falling for him.

"Okay, God, it's time You and I had a talk." She poured a fresh cup of coffee and limped outside to sit on the stool in the back of the building where she could be alone with her thoughts.

Where had all these soft mushy feelings for Ben come from? What would she do about them?

And why didn't God help Rose's Roses?

She pushed her glasses up and heard Ben's voice again. *What if you didn't have that excuse?*

"It's even better than you said it would be." Ben walked around his yard, appreciating the many details Jayne had incorporated. "The sculptures are perfect."

"Of course they are. Too bad you weren't here when they were delivered."

"Uh-huh." Ben had deliberately avoided meeting Cass again after hearing from Jerry last night. Someone was doing a lot of poking into David Bentley's existence.

"The church had some money donated for Cass to create something. She has an idea for the Easter service. She's going to phone you," Jayne said.

"Great." So much for avoidance.

"The fountains look good, don't you think?"

"Everything looks wonderful. You've done extremely well." Her shoulder bumped his as she stepped awkwardly. Ben assisted her then lifted a gleaming auburn strand from the corner of her mouth. "I insist on taking you and Emma to dinner to celebrate."

"Oh." He thought she'd refuse, but after a moment Jayne nodded. "Thank you. That would be nice."

He arranged for a time to pick them up then stood watching

as she drove away. Though he'd added a hefty bonus to her check, Ben had overheard a conversation she'd had with Sidney this afternoon in which they'd commiserated over how tough things were at Rose's Roses. It left Ben dubious that even his bonus would be enough to solve her current financial woes. That made Ben wary. Was it possible Jayne knew of David Bentley's true identity and saw Ben as an answer to her troubles? Ben's imagination exploded and he began to imagine all sorts of scenarios in which Jayne knew his identity as an author and would exploit that knowledge. Whoa! Reality called a halt to his imaginings while his heart questioned even thinking such a thing of her.

Cass. Jayne. You're suspicious of everyone. Could it be because you feel guilty for not telling Jayne the truth? Especially when you've pushed her so hard to face her own truths.

His nagging conscience was bang on. Ben had begun to hate the deception he'd worked so hard to create, but that didn't make it any less necessary. Never again did he want to find out someone he cared about was using him.

So you care about her.

As more than just a friend. And that's what worried him the most.

He heard his own words echo in the afternoon's silence. *Life doesn't come with guarantees. Once in a while you have to take a risk and trust God to work it out.*

He cared about Jayne. A lot. He didn't want there to be any secrets between them. She was creative and beautiful and generous and loving—and he was almost certain she was the woman God had brought him to Palm Springs to meet. Almost.

Yet a nugget of distrust buried deep in his heart still left him wary.

Jayne needed money to keep her business afloat.

Ben made a decision.

He'd wait. He'd spend time praying for God to make his will clear, and he'd do whatever he could to help Jayne. By Easter he'd surely know enough about her to either pursue the relationship or not.

And speaking of Easter, he was overdue to help with the set painting. Tonight at dinner, he'd push for concrete plans from Emma and Jayne about the flowers. Today he knew his path.

Ben was going to wait for God to unfold his future. He only hoped some nosy busybody didn't spoil it.

"It's been a lovely evening," Emma said, smiling. "I don't know when I've enjoyed such a tasty meal."

"I don't know when I've eaten with two such beautiful women." Ben squeezed Emma's hand, but his smile rested on Jayne. "You both look lovely."

She shifted under that smile, reveling in the warmth of it and the way it made her feel. Tonight she wasn't clumsy and uncomfortable. Tonight she felt pretty and womanly in the turquoise dress Ben said matched her eyes.

"I'm so glad you clarified the Easter plans. Jayne and I want to coordinate our part completely, even though she's had to miss meetings. Thank you, Ben." Emma patted his hand. "But now I think I should go home. I'm a bit weary."

Having watched gray shadows creep into those beloved eyes, Jayne quickly agreed as she gathered her shawl.

"You two shouldn't disrupt your evening." Emma pretended to peer in her purse for something. "The tramway has a late-night car up the mountain. Ben's never seen it, have you?"

"No," he admitted.

"Why don't you and Jayne take a ride up there? It's such a lovely night."

"Granny," Jayne protested, but Ben overrode her.

"It would be great to share it with you, Jayne."

Privately, she thought so, too. They made Emma comfortable at the condo, Jayne found a heavier wrap then Ben drove up the hill to the boarding area.

"It will be cold up there," Jayne warned. "Bring your jacket."

Only a few people were around. They shared the tramcar with one other couple, an elderly pair who held hands all the way up. On arrival, the old man escorted the woman as they exited the tram with tender care then folded her arm through his as they strolled around the outside viewing platform.

"That's what I want," Ben murmured as they trailed behind the two seniors.

"What?" Jayne looked around in confusion.

"That. A timeless love like theirs."

"They could be newlyweds," she teased. "We get lots of those in Palm Springs."

"No." Ben shook his head. "Look at the way he escorts her, close enough to help or lean on. Dependable."

"And her?"

"She knows he won't let her trip or fall. They've gone through lots of things together and she knows this man, knows he will keep her from harm. They trust each other." He looked at her, his eyes dark and moody. "That's the kind of love I want."

Jayne didn't know what to say to that, so she pretended to study the snow piled up around a huge rock just beyond the fence. The snow would hang around till late spring, she knew. Maybe longer in the cracks and crannies where the sun didn't reach.

"You're awfully quiet."

"I was thinking about Easter. This will be the twelfth anniversary of my parents' deaths."

"I'm sorry." His hand found hers and squeezed. But he didn't let go. "It must be hard to celebrate on that day."

"It's getting easier." Jayne quelled the riot in her stomach by drawing her hand away on the pretext of moving to a bench which overlooked the valley below. "Easter celebrations in Heaven must be so much more exciting than ours. I think of my parents there and it gets easier."

"Do you think our choir will ever master the 'Hallelujah Chorus'?" Ben asked. He sat down beside her and chuckled. "I heard them this afternoon. There are a couple of voices who will never achieve those high notes."

"It's the thought that counts. There's the wind farm you were talking about the other day," she said, pointing across the valley. "I wish someone would infuse me with energy."

"Problems?" Ben leaned back and laid his arm across the bench, behind her shoulders.

"Same old. Same old. I've got to figure out a way to up our income." She shook her head. "Sorry. I don't want to be a downer."

"You're not. I'd like to help."

"Thanks, but I think this is something I have to do on my own." She was going to say more but two men who were on the deck above them stood whispering and pointing. "Do you know them?" she asked, surprised by Ben's frown.

"No." He rose, held out a hand. "You must be frozen. It's cold out here. Want to go upstairs and get some coffee."

"Sure." Jayne took his hand. They climbed the stairs together. "There's our couple," she said, inclining her head toward the elderly pair they'd noticed earlier. "Still holding hands."

"So are—" Ben stopped speaking when a man stepped in front of him.

"Excuse me? Are you Da—?"

"Ben Cummings." Ben stared at the two. "Do I know you?"

"Cummings?" One man glanced at the other. They both shook their heads. "No. Sorry to bother you." As they walked away, Jayne heard one man say, "I told you it wasn't him."

"Who do you suppose they thought you were?" she asked curiously.

"No clue." He led her to a table.

"But this has happened before."

He shrugged. "Guess I have that kind of face. Now will you have tea or coffee?"

"Tea, please." She watched him move toward the counter. Ben didn't have a common kind of face. Not at all. "It seems strange that people keep mistaking you," she murmured when he returned with their drinks and two small pastries.

"I guess. But there's nothing I can do about it." He nodded. "Look at our couple."

They had turned their chairs to stare out the window and were sitting with their heads leaning against each other's.

"A match made in Heaven," she whispered.

"That's where they should all be made," Ben said.

He was oddly quiet for the rest of the evening. As he walked to Emma's condo, he mentioned that his birthday was the following Tuesday.

"How will you celebrate?" she asked.

"Same as usual. Buy myself a German chocolate cake and pig out. Maybe swim some laps and see a movie." They'd reached Emma's. "Thank you for showing me the mountain, Jayne. It was fun."

"It was my pleasure. And thank you for the dinner. And the job. You were a pretty good first client."

"Liar." He laughed at her blush. "I hope it's only the first time we celebrate completion of your landscaping. I'll certainly spread the word."

"Thanks." She didn't know what else to say, so to cover the awkward moment, Jayne drew out her keys and slid them into the lock. "Well, good—"

Ben kissed her.

And when her knees started wobbling and her stomach danced cartwheels and her brain screamed for more, he lifted his head, pressed a second kiss against her forehead and eased her into Emma's condo.

"Good night, Jayne," he whispered before he closed the door.

Chapter Eight

The following day Ben dived into a new chapter of David Bentley's latest work and was well and truly buried in the story when the doorbell broke his concentration.

Muttering dire threats, he yanked open the door and blinked.

"Emma! Is anything wrong?"

"Lots of things." She stepped inside and closed the door. "You and I need to have a chat, young man."

"Okay." What was this about? "Would like a cup of coffee—tea?" he substituted, remembering she was supposed to limit caffeine. "Herbal."

"Fine." She walked beside him to the kitchen and sat down at the granite breakfast bar. "This is a nice house. I suppose David Bentley can afford it."

Ben froze for a second. He finished filling the kettle and set it to boil. He took out two cups and the tea. Then there was nothing to do but face Jayne's grandmother.

"Does Jayne know?"

"No. And I can't help wondering why that is. Why haven't you told her the truth about yourself, Ben, or David, or whoever you are?"

"Allan Benjamin Cummings is my legal name. David Bentley is a pseudonym I created."

"Was that so hard?" Emma demanded. She slid off her stool and went to turn off the boiling kettle. She poured water in the cups, added tea bags to both then handed him one. "Why haven't you said that to Jayne?"

"Emma, I've spent years keeping my identity as David Bentley a secret. You have no idea how intrusive it can be." He motioned her to a seat. "I had a good reason. It gave me some privacy and it didn't hurt anyone. So when I met Jayne…" Ben shrugged. "But I will tell her."

"You had better do it soon." There was a note of worry underlying Emma's words.

"What's the rush? It's no big deal. It's just a name I write under. I am still Ben Cummings."

"It's a very big deal. To Jayne." Emma sighed. "Did she ever tell you about her high school days?"

"Some. She had a rough time of it, I gather."

"She was miserable. I tried my best, but there were two girls at school who reveled in hurting her, putting her down. They made her recovery and her life in that school as difficult as possible." Emma's lips pursed but she continued. "I kept telling Jayne to pray for them, to let God handle them, not to let her spirit get beaten by them."

"Not bad advice."

"I should have spanked them."

He smothered a smile. "What happened?"

"Two months before school ended, these two girls apologized to Jayne. They asked her to be part of their group. They took her to their parties. They even helped her find her graduation dress. They invited her to their homes. In short they became her best friends and she trusted them."

Emma paused. Ben said nothing, content to let her tell the story her own way.

"Jayne had this problem with balance. It was infinitely worse when her knee clicked out. She was waiting until graduation was over to have her last surgery." Emma stared at him, tears welling in her beautiful eyes. "Graduation was a big deal in this school, long fancy gowns and a formal ceremony in which the graduates walked up a set of stairs onto a stage to accept their diplomas. Then they came down the stairs in a parade of graduates. Jayne was sure she could trust them so she confided in her *friends* about her knee. They offered to help her master going up and down the stairs."

Emma stopped. The silence grew loud and ominous.

"What happened?" Ben had a terrible sinking feeling.

"As Jayne was coming down the stairs that night, one of them stepped on the hem of her dress. She lost her balance, her knee buckled and she fell. The girls had planned it all. They'd doctored her dress so the seam was weak. The bottom of her skirt tore away." Tears flowed down Emma's cheeks. "They'd told everyone they were going to do it. They all stood there and laughed at her. Not one of those kids helped Jayne."

Anger surged up inside. Ben had seen this kind of cruelty in his own school. But he'd never been targeted like this.

"A night that should have been a wonderful memory turned into a nightmare. It took her months to leave the house after the operation. She'd hoped to go away to school but that fell through, too. It's taken ages for her to come out of her shell. Taking your landscaping job on is the furthest she's ever gone."

"But I haven't done anything like that to Jayne," he protested.

"Haven't you? How do you think Jayne's going to feel when people find out who you are? Her clients are her friends. Don't you think she's going to feel stupid and used when they keep asking why she didn't know who you were? Do you think she'll trust you if she finds out from someone else who you are?" Emma squeezed his arm, her tone fierce. "I will not allow my granddaughter to be hurt like that again. If you care about her at all, you have to tell her, Ben."

"I care about her. I think I love her." He bit his lip, wishing he'd remained silent.

"You only 'think' you love her?" Emma laughed. It emerged a harsh sharp sound. "That's not enough. Not for my Jayne."

Ben didn't know what to say. He didn't want to tell her his reason for waiting. Emma would rage at him for daring to believe her beloved granddaughter would want his money. But Ben needed to know that for himself.

"Let me tell you what love is, Ben. Love is strong. It's patient and kind. It isn't proud or jealous or envious. Love isn't selfish. I Corinthians 13 says it best. 'If you love someone you will be loyal to him no matter what the cost. You will always believe in him, always expect the best of him and always stand your ground in defending him.'" The tiny woman rose. "That's the kind of love Jayne deserves. The kind of love that doesn't hide behind secrets and pretend, but comes out strong, the kind that's there when you need it. The kind of love you can depend on, no matter what."

She walked toward the front door. Ben followed, stopped when she paused at the entrance.

"My granddaughter has been hurt so many times. Please don't let it happen again."

Then Emma was gone in the cab that had brought her.

Ben watched it leave. He remembered the old couple from the tramway. Dependable. Trustworthy. Loyal. Those were the things that made love strong. Money had nothing to do with it.

He'd told Emma he thought he loved Jayne. That wasn't the truth.

The truth was Ben knew he loved Jayne Rose. Fiercely, protectively. Totally.

Back in his office, Ben glanced at the calendar. Two weeks until Easter. According to Jerry, the mystery of David Bentley's identity had now been taken up by other tabloid reporters. Ben had to tell Jayne the truth before one of them broke the story.

He'd make it a special occasion, he decided. A night to remember. He'd tell her about David, explain his reasons. Then he'd tell her he loved her.

It was time to trust God completely now.

Ben Cummings loved Jayne Rose. She was the woman God had sent.

Jayne stood at the counter in Rose's Roses, with the phone to her ear, and listened, hardly daring to believe it was true.

"And because you saw what I did for Ben, you want me to do your landscaping?" she repeated.

The woman's voice confirmed it.

"I'll have to see the place first, judge what I can do with the space. I'll also need some time to decide on whether I can take on another job right away." The conversation had escalated Jayne's niggling doubts into full-blown shivers.

They settled on a time to talk again and Jayne hung up, stunned by this answer to prayer. But could she do it?

A hand on her shoulder startled her from her reverie.

"Where were you?" Ben teased, his grin wide. "I've called your name three times."

"Sorry." She had to share her news. "I've been offered a new job, a landscaping job. Cass told a woman about your yard. She liked it and has offered me the job."

"Hey! I told you to have faith. God sure came through for you. Congratulations." He hugged her. "This calls for a celebration. Tonight. What time should I pick you up?"

"Oh. I'm not sure Emma can come. She has a meeting."

"Then you and I'll go. Seven?"

Bemused, Jayne nodded. Ben kissed her cheek then hurried toward the door, muttering about set builders.

"Oh," he called, pausing in the doorway. "You'd better make sure there are lots of plants and flowers ordered for the Easter service. The sets they've created are massive."

"Don't worry. We've planned a lovely *expandable* garden setting."

"What happens to the flowers after?" he asked.

"They go to different nursing homes and hospitals. What should I wear—for tonight?"

"Doesn't matter. You're always beautiful. See you later." He grinned and was gone.

Sidney was out delivering and Emma hadn't come in today. So Jayne stood among the fragrant hyacinth and thought about Ben. He was so nice, so generous. She felt safe with him. She could trust Ben with anything. He'd never let her down.

That's how she felt about God, now, too. Over and over He'd come through for her. She was desperate for income, but the deposit on the new landscape project would tide them over a little longer. She could trust Him. He wouldn't let her down.

She adjusted her new glasses and started work on an arrangement. Then it hit her. If she trusted God, why wasn't she willing to have the operation? God had taken care of them this far. He wasn't going to abandon her now.

Ben would say it was time to put her faith to the test.

Ben was a smart man.

Jayne picked up the phone and dialed.

"Could you tell Dr. Smith I'd like to speak to him about that operation?"

She'd barely hung up the phone when it rang again.

"Jayne?" The Realtor she'd listed Rose's Roses with

sounded excited. "I think I've found a buyer for Rose's Roses. Can we meet with you tonight?"

She hated to cancel dinner, but maybe selling was God telling her to trust Him and take another step. Besides, she had a hunch Ben would make another date soon.

Imagine her, Jayne Rose, going on a date.

The embers inside glowed a little warmer. She hugged herself and relished the rush of joy that always spurted up inside whenever she thought about Ben.

"Thank You for sending him, God."

Chapter Nine

"So you're not going to take the offer to buy Rose's Roses?" Two days later Ben had coaxed Jayne to share lunch with him after church because he knew Emma would be enjoying a meal with friends.

Though Jayne and he had finished eating, they remained seated in the outdoor café, enjoying the light breezes.

"No, I'm not."

"Why not? It would free you to concentrate on landscaping." Ben loved the way her face lit up and gave her that translucent inner glow. Everyone should feel so happy about their jobs, he thought, wondering if it was egotistical to think he might have something to do with this new verve and vitality she radiated.

"I don't have enough landscaping experience or jobs to make it my whole focus right now," Jayne explained. She savored the last spoonful of her lime sherbet. "But more importantly, Emma still wants to work at the shop. Not as many hours and only a bit till she's fully recovered, but her being there would be a real help for me while I expand."

"Expand? But I thought you didn't have the money."

"I didn't. But—" Jayne nudged her glasses an inch higher, her smile widening "—I cashed in the life insurance policy Granny Em bought after my parents died. If I don't do too much at once, that money should keep things stable for a while."

"Very clever," he applauded. His heart almost sang at the answer to his prayer. Now he knew that Jayne wasn't looking for the easy solution to her problems.

Jayne could have sold out and used the money to plow ahead with her dream, but she put her grandmother first. And she'd found the resourcefulness to ensure their business future. This was not a woman looking for easy money. She valued people.

More than ever Ben was certain Jayne was the woman for him.

"Jayne, I need to tell you something—"

"I have another surprise—"

The looked at each other and laughed.

"You first," Ben said gallantly.

"My surprise is…" She paused, with a smile. "I've decided to have the surgery. It's the day after tomorrow."

"Really?" Another answered prayer.

"It's all thanks to you," Jayne told him, her face alive and happy. "You helped me face my fears. You taught me to trust God and push ahead. You helped me see that my past doesn't determine my future. So thank you, Ben."

"I didn't do anything."

"Yes, you did. You're the first person I've trusted in a long time. That's a very big something. And I'm grateful." She smiled at him. "What were you going to say?"

He couldn't tell her the truth now. Not when she needed to focus on her operation. But he could tell her right afterward. He could arrange a special meal with candles and flowers. He'd make sure they had privacy and then he'd tell her who he was and that he loved her.

"Ben? What were you going to say?"

"Never mind." He grinned. "I'll tell you later. Are you ready to take a look at those sets for the Easter service?"

"Sure."

She rose, but before they could leave a young man approached. Ben took Jayne's arm to steer her aside, but the man was persistent.

"Excuse me. Are you—?"

"This is Jayne and I'm Ben. Ben Cummings. Do we know you?"

"Ben?" The man frowned.

"That's me." Ben waited a fraction of a moment then shrugged. "Well, excuse us. We have to go."

"Ben Cummings?"

"Yeah."

"Oh." The man remained in place, staring at him.

"Let's go, Ben." Jayne curled her arm into his and they walked away. "How many times is this going to happen, do you suppose? It's weird."

Ben said nothing. He and Jayne spent the afternoon with the committee, hammering out the last details for the Easter service to be held in two weeks.

"Will your eyes be healed enough by then?" he asked during a coffee break.

"The doctor says I only need to stay overnight in the hospital after the surgery. No heavy lifting afterward and sunglasses outside. Otherwise, life as usual."

They made a very quick trip to Cass's to see the cross she was making for Easter. After the service it would be permanently installed outside the church. Later they stopped by the condo. Emma was asleep and a friend was making dinner, so Ben invited Jayne for a swim in his pool. She fit at his house. She belonged there. And he wondered how long it would be before she agreed to marry him. He was going to court her like a queen. Because she was. His queen.

Jayne was every bit as good a swimmer as Ben, her knee no problem in the buoyant water. Her laughter rang through the kitchen as she helped him prepare a barbecue feast. And later, when they sat on the pool deck, under the stars, talking about her operation, shoulders rubbing, it seemed perfectly normal for Ben to cradle her hand in his.

"I have to go home," Jayne murmured finally. "I have so much to do tomorrow."

"Okay." He drew her to her feet, wrapped his arms around her and held her close enough that he could whisper in her ear. "You're a strong, beautiful woman, Jayne Rose. You're going to come through that operation with flying colors."

"God willing," she agreed. Her hands rested on his shoulders.

"I know He is." Ben rested his chin on her head and recited, "'O God, my Strength! I will sing your praises, for you are my place of safety. My God is changeless in his love for me.'"

"Another Psalm." Jayne tipped her head back and smiled. "You really admire David's songs, don't you?"

"He is my Biblical hero," Ben said. "I strive to be as secure in my faith as he was."

"I'm going to, too."

"Jayne, about earlier. I wanted to tell you—"

She placed a finger across his lips.

"Could it wait, Ben? Please? I really need to get home."

"Sure. No problem." He could wait to tell her about David Bentley. But as he studied her beautiful face in the moonlight, Ben wasn't quite ready to let Jayne leave his embrace. Instead he bent his head and placed his lips against hers.

After a tiny gasp, Jayne returned his kiss, her hands tightening around his neck, drawing him closer.

This was the right woman. Ben knew it as certainly as he knew his name.

"This is lovely," she whispered. "But I really do have to go."

"Yes, you do," he agreed, releasing her. He would say nothing about what was in his heart until he could tell her the whole truth. "May I be there while you're having surgery?"

"I'd be disappointed if you weren't," she said shyly.

So Ben drove her home, walked her to her door and thoroughly kissed her good-night.

"Sleep well."

But as he returned to his home through the sparkling lights of the desert at night, Ben knew time was running short for him. That man this afternoon had emphasized the fact that Ben's cover could be blown at any time. And when he pressed the answering machine button, Jerry reinforced that with a phone message.

"They're getting close, Ben. Don't be surprised if someone shows up and sandbags you when you least expect it. I don't know how, but your information is getting out. Be careful."

Ben didn't sleep that night. He kept seeing Jayne's face, glowing in the sunlight when she told him she trusted him.

"Don't let anyone spoil that," he prayed as dark turned to dawn.

One more day. And then she'd know the truth.

"Ready?" Ben asked, holding Jayne's hand tightly as the staff waited to wheel her away.

"Yes." But her big beautiful eyes, now bare of the thick lenses, held shadows. "Pray, will you, Ben?"

"Nonstop," he assured her.

"I have a verse for you," she said, her smile tremulous. "'O God, my heart is quiet and confident.' I like David's faith."

"Me, too." He bent and kissed her.

"We have to go now," the nurse said.

Ben nodded, gave Jayne's hand one last squeeze and stepped back. The nurses whisked her away. Ben dialed Emma.

"She's just gone in."

"I'm praying," Emma said. "Did you tell her yet?"

"Tonight. I'm having a meal catered. I've got Sidney bringing flowers." He had to share his happiness. "I'm going to tell her something else, too," he murmured.

"I'm glad."

They said goodbye. Ben went to the chapel to ask for some heavenly help. This was going to be the most important night of his life.

The bandages made it impossible to know who was coming and going from her room, so Jayne called out each time she heard a footstep. But the answer was never the one she wanted to hear.

Where was Ben?

The grogginess had dissipated quickly. She felt good, pain-free and hopeful. A nurse dialed the phone so Jayne could talk to her grandmother.

"I'm back, Granny. The doctor said everything went well."

"I knew it would, dear. I've been praying."

"Thank you." Jayne bit her bottom lip, debating. "Granny, do you know where Ben is?"

"He was there. He phoned to tell me when you went in for surgery." Emma's beloved voice sounded troubled. "I can't imagine he'd have left."

"No." But Jayne's doubt would not be quashed despite the inner voice that cheered *Have some faith*.

"I'm sure he'll turn up soon," Emma murmured.

"Yes." Jayne forced a laugh. "Somebody's probably way-laid him again, thinking he's someone else."

Emma's silence bothered her, but Jayne decided her grandmother must be tired. Promising to call later, she said goodbye and hung up. She dozed off, dreaming of Ben, and woke to warm lips pressed against her temple.

"Hey," he said softly. "How are you?"

"Fine." She held up a hand, relieved when his fingers threaded through hers. "I wondered where you were."

"It's embarrassing," he said, humor lacing his voice. "I fell asleep while I was praying in the chapel. I didn't get much rest last night."

"Didn't take your own advice, huh?" She grinned. "To trust in God, I mean."

"You're right." He brushed her hair away from her face, touched her cheek. "Jayne, I have something special planned for this evening. I know you'll still have your bandages on, but the doctor said you'll be able to get up."

"Of course I will. I feel fine. Just dopey."

"Well, you rest this afternoon and tonight I'll share my surprise." His voice dropped. "I need to tell you something. Two somethings."

A fizzle of delight worked its way through her body. Maybe he was going to tell her he loved her. Because Jayne knew beyond a shadow of a doubt that she loved Ben. She'd known for sure when she was lying on the stretcher, on her way to surgery, and he kissed her. It hadn't happened with fireworks, the way she'd expected. It was simply a sweet quiet knowledge that filled her soul.

Ben was the one.

"You're tired," he whispered. "Sleep, Jayne. We'll talk later." His lips brushed hers and then, with a whoosh of air, she knew he was gone.

To arrange his surprise.

"Thank You, God," she breathed.

She did sleep a little, dozing off and on. Sidney stopped

by with some flowers and a huge vase which she said Ben had sent. Jayne knew by the touch and scent that they were roses.

"Red," Sidney confirmed. "Long stems. A dozen. I've put them right beside you so you can enjoy their fragrance."

"Thank you." Jayne breathed deeply as the fizzy feeling sent an effervescent wash along her nerves. Red roses meant love.

"My pleasure." Sidney laughed. "Everything's fine at the shop. You rest and get better so you can come back to work soon."

"Yes, ma'am."

At five-thirty someone from a catering company arrived and set up a table. Jayne heard the clink of dishes, crystal and silver. She was imagining what it looked like when Cass arrived.

"Wow! Celebrating already." She hugged Jayne and handed her a small box. Inside was a metal sculpture.

"A lion?" Jayne guessed, feeling the cool surface.

"Because you have the heart of a lion," Cass said. They'd discovered they shared the same faith when Cass delivered Ben's sculptures and Cass had been full of questions about him ever since. "Here's Ben."

"Hello," Jayne heard him say. But there was a tight reserve in his voice that did not sound welcoming.

"Hi, yourself. How's the book coming?"

Book? Jayne frowned.

"Fine."

She wanted to ask questions but Cass beat her to it.

"There's quite a furor about you in Los Angeles, Ben. Wouldn't it be better to announce your identity as David Bentley, rather than allow some exposé about your pseudonym?"

In that instant, the pieces fell into place. Ben was David Bentley. The books in his office, the secretive way he'd talked about his business, the people who kept recognizing him—it all made sense.

"Well, it looks like you two have planned a fancy dinner. I'll leave. Take care," Cass said, hugging Jayne.

"You, too. Thanks for the lion." Heart of a lion? More like the brain of a donkey. How could she not have known?

The door clicked closed.

"Jayne—"

"You lied to me. Over and over, you lied to me." She gulped down the tears and let anger take over. "I should never have trusted you."

"Jayne, listen. I love you. I was going to tell you everything tonight. That's why I arranged—"

"Love me?" She laughed as scornfully as her bleeding heart would allow. "You don't deceive people you love, Ben. Or David. Whoever you are."

"I didn't deceive you. I am Ben Cummings. Always have been." He tried to take her hand but she yanked it away. "I've wanted to tell you so many times."

"I trusted you." She was glad she couldn't look at him, glad the bandages wouldn't let the tears out.

"And you still can. I haven't done anything wrong. I am Ben Cummings. David Bentley is just a name I use on my books. It doesn't mean anything."

"It means everything." She was so stupid, so gullible. How could she have let herself be betrayed again? "You've been pretending. All the time we've spent together, you've been acting a part because you couldn't or wouldn't trust me with the truth. Why?"

"I've learned not to tell people about David Bentley," he said, a grim tone in his voice. "It's safer that way."

"Safer for whom? You? Because you won't have to sign some autographs?" Jayne shook her head. "Not good enough. You said we were friends. You said friends help friends. Is this your idea of help? When would I have been trustworthy,

Ben? When would you have told me the truth about who you really are?"

"Tonight. I had it all arranged to tell you tonight."

"Sure," she sneered. "Do you know how stupid I feel? All those people who kept stopping you. All the times you cut them off, pretended they had the wrong person. I did your yard. Do you think anyone is going to believe I didn't know who you are? So now you've made me part of your lie."

"I didn't intend that. I only wanted time to get to know you, time to find out—"

"Whether I was worthy of being part of your world?" Jayne sagged, all her energy depleted by a gaping wound of hurt that no amount of surgery could fix. "Did Emma know?" she asked as understanding dawned.

"She guessed."

"Go away, Ben. Leave and don't come back."

"You don't mean that. You can't," he pleaded, his hand grabbing hers. "I love you, Jayne."

"You don't know what love means. You want to work it and shape it to meet your needs. You use people. You used me. That's what I can't forgive, Ben." She pulled back. "Please leave."

"I do love you, Jayne." He let her go, stepped back. His voice sounded anguished. "You'll never know how long and how hard I prayed that you would be the woman I searched for."

"But you didn't have any faith in me. You preached to me about trusting God, but you didn't trust God or me. You kept up your deception until it suited your purposes. That's what I can't forgive." She sighed. "I should have expected it, I suppose. It's not the first time I've been deceived." But this hurt far more than high school.

"Jayne—"

"Just go. I don't want to hear any more stories. Leave me

alone." She leaned back against her pillows and turned her head aside.

"I have been totally truthful about one thing, Jayne. I do love you."

She kept her face averted until she heard the door close behind him.

Only then did she let the tears flow, uncaring when they seeped between the bandages and streamed down her cheeks.

Why, God? I trusted You. I believed You had my best interests in mind. How is this best?

The faith she'd worked so hard to build was now caught in an internal struggle that had never really gone away.

She was the outsider. She didn't fit in.

Never had.

Never would.

Chapter Ten

Groveling was something Ben Cummings had never done. But he was more than willing to do it now if it helped Jayne forgive him. Five days without talking to her was driving him nuts. She wouldn't take his calls, but she couldn't run out of the store.

Could she?

After pacing outside Rose's Roses for five minutes, he took a deep breath and pushed open the door. Jayne lifted her head, free of bandages and the cumbersome glasses. She surveyed him with those magnificent stormy aqua eyes, and left the sales floor.

He felt a rush of relief. She must have regained her sight.

"Hi, Ben." Emma sat behind the worktable. She stopped adding sprays of flowers to the huge vase in front of her and offered him a tentative smile. "How are you?"

"Fine, Emma. Thanks." He got the message her eyes telegraphed. *I told you so.*

"What can I help you with?"

"The Easter decorating. It's only four days away." That wasn't the reason he'd come in, but he'd use it if it would get Jayne to talk to him. "We've changed things a bit and since Jayne missed our last meeting—"

"We are not changing anything for our part in the Easter display." Jayne marched out from the back, her eyes the color of a tempest in the tropics. "We're busy. We can't be altering our arrangements just because you've decided to change something. This is our livelihood, not a game."

"I realize that. I only wanted to tell you that the pastor insists we add something to Cass's cross that sits in the background." He let his gaze feast on her lovely face. "I know we'd decided no potted lilies for the display because they weren't historically correct, but the latest decision is to order two."

"Fine." She grabbed an order form, scrawled "two lilies" across it and smashed it on the metal spoke that held a pile of other orders. "Anything else?"

"Jayne," he murmured, for her ears alone, "I really am sorry. I never meant—"

"Yes, you did. Or you would have spoken the truth the first time someone stopped you." She glared at him. "All those people who stopped you must have thought I knew you were David Bentley. I feel so stupid. And embarrassed."

"I know, but—"

"You didn't have enough faith in me, Ben. Not in me and not in God. You who were always telling me to trust, to believe God could handle anything." She shifted off her bad leg. "Why didn't you take your own advice?"

"I should have."

"Yes. Instead, once more I'm the outsider, the one who was never let in on the joke, the butt of everyone's laughter."

"No one's laughing, Jayne." Certainly not him.

"You're living like a coward, Ben. Which makes me wonder—what are you so afraid of?" She shook her head angrily. "I don't care. Just go. Leave us alone. We'll do the flowers on Easter. But after that, I don't want to see you again."

"Jayne, please. Let me explain."

"You're too late." She turned and walked away.

Ben stood there for several minutes, hoping, praying, she'd change her mind. But she didn't. And there was nothing more he could say.

He waved to Emma and walked out the door. Jayne was furious at him. He didn't blame her. But now he began to wonder if her fury would extend to telling the media about him.

Suddenly his phone rang.

"I found the culprit, Ben." Jerry sounded angry. "I've stopped what I could, but I can't guarantee you're in the clear. Maybe you should think about moving again."

Ben closed his phone, sat on a park bench and did just that—he thought. Was that what he wanted, to move again, to be continually looking behind his back, wondering? Was the price of anonymity really worth what it was costing him? Was it worth losing Jayne, the woman God had sent into his life? The woman he loved?

What are you afraid of?

He wasn't afraid. Was he?

But that's exactly what he was. It was the reason he'd misjudged Jayne a few moments ago. He knew her, knew she didn't care about status or money. He'd seen that over and over in the way she dealt with her clients, in her dedication to her landscaping, in the intricate details she added to every order. Jayne cared about people. She cared that her grandmother had a place to feel needed; she cared so much she was willing to adjust her own plans.

Jayne was hurting and angry, but she wasn't vindictive. She wasn't going to run to the press with what she knew. He could trust her. He should have trusted her. She was right. He hadn't trusted God, either. Well, that was over.

Ben prayed for forgiveness and wisdom then dialed his phone.

"Jerry, I want you to arrange a party here at the convention center for Saturday night."

"A party for what?"

"To reveal the identity of David Bentley."

His lawyer and friend gave a whoop of joy before he hung up.

Ben walked to his car. He'd tell whoever wanted to know that he was David Bentley and deal with the consequences. But Ben was also going to tell the world that he loved Jayne Rose.

Saturday's flurry of business didn't stop until well after six. Jayne forced herself through the day, wondering how she would deal with seeing Ben tomorrow, Easter morning.

"You've been moping around too long. You need to see these." Emma dropped a file of photocopied newspaper clippings on her desk. "Sidney and I got them from the library. Maybe they'll help you understand his reasons. Read them. Sidney's taking me home."

When the front door lock clicked, Jayne reached for the folder and surveyed the first page. She read about a young Benjamin Cummings who had been left a fortune, but lost his father. She read of his five-day long abduction and the huge ransom that had been grudgingly paid by his guardian. She read of the money said guardian had embezzled and the very public court case that followed. She saw pictures of young bewildered Ben being jostled by reporters who tracked him down no matter where he went. There were later pictures of him with a young woman and a host of prying, personal stories about Ben's net worth. There were also articles on the woman's claim that Ben loved money more than her because he wouldn't give her money.

Then a lag in time and the clippings focused on David Bentley's first bestseller. There were numerous pieces about the fans, kind and crazy, who began stalking him. There were photos of an injured Ben after being attacked by a woman on the street, a report of a break-in at his home and several other incidents. Then the articles died off. David Bentley had gone underground. The books, wonderful, endearing funny suspense novels that enchanted readers from teens to seniors, kept coming, but David Bentley became an enigma.

At the very bottom of the file, Jayne found an announcement that David Bentley would meet the public tonight.

Ben was going to tell the world who he was.

Jayne absorbed the impact of that. Then she leaned back in her chair to think. She now knew why Ben hadn't told her who he was. She imagined a child of ten being hidden for five long days only to learn that the one person he could trust had betrayed him. She understood his craving for privacy, his need to be in control, his reason for keeping his secret. But she also realized it didn't matter.

The truth was plain and simple. Jayne loved Ben. It didn't matter if he wrote books as someone else. Nothing mattered but the fact that she'd trusted God and He'd sent her a man who filled her dreams, a man who forced her to think about her decisions and make a change, a man who helped her reach for her dreams and accomplish them. A man who encouraged her to keep dreaming bigger and better things while trusting God to help her accomplish them.

Ben taught her that God is a God of can do, not afraid to do. He helped her see that she had to face her fears in order to be able to reach for her dreams. He'd helped her understand that living with failure is easier than never reaching for what you want.

Was she prepared to give up a man like that because she was afraid to trust him again?

No! The word exploded from her heart.

Jayne jumped to her feet, grabbed her purse and keys. Forgiveness was a two-way street. She'd been wrong not to listen to his explanation. With God's help she would not let fear cost her the man who owned her heart.

With barely half an hour before the event started, Jayne had to get to the convention center. Unfortunately, the big clunky van wouldn't start. She hailed a taxi and sat back, praying as hard as she ever had. She called Emma and asked her to pray, too.

On arriving at the center, Jayne hurried in under the big sweeping roof, pushed her way through the glass doors and stopped. Where would Ben be?

Lord?

An acquaintance who often helped cater events at the center stood beside a sign indicating Ben's event would take place in the ballroom. Jayne explained her mission. Together they created a diversion to lure away security while Jayne pushed her way into Ben's room.

"I'm sorry, you can't come in here— Jayne?" Ben waved away the guard who had hold of her arm, closed the door. "What are you doing here?"

"We need to talk."

"I've wanted to do that for days," he said, his voice low. "I want to apologize. I should have told you the truth. I know that now."

"Yes, you should have," she said quietly. "But you didn't. Emma showed me some old clippings. I think I understand why."

"You do?" Relief mingled with confusion. "Then?"

"I understand you were wary about me, Ben. You've had some pretty awful experiences. So have I. But the thing is, I love you." There, she'd said it. Jayne held out a hand as Ben moved forward. "Wait. I have to say this."

"I'm listening." He sat on a chair, his gaze riveted on her. "Go ahead."

"For so long I've been the outsider. It didn't seem to matter what I did, I couldn't fit in. I was always the oddball. And by not telling me, you made me feel even more that way." She swallowed. "You said you loved me."

"I do."

"Then if you love me, you can't treat me like an outsider anymore. I don't care about your money, Ben. Money comes and goes. But love doesn't. It's not your money I want. It's your love."

"You've got it." He rose and began slowly walking toward her.

"You came and you filled my heart. You were my gift from God. I refuse to let that gift go to waste," she said.

"Good." Ben slid his arms around her waist and studied her face. "Because you are my gift, too. I've prayed for years for God to send me a special woman who I could spend the rest of my life with, one who would love me and not the money. You are that woman."

"Are you sure?"

"Positive. The money's an albatross, Jayne. It causes distrust. It gets in the way. It interfered with my trust in God, and in my love for you."

"The money doesn't matter, Ben," she assured him. "Except that I have nothing to give you to make you believe that. I could sign a prenuptial if that would help you believe me, or sign some statement that I don't want anything from you. That's the only way I have to prove that I love you, not your money or things."

"Dearest Jayne." He lifted her arms and draped them around his neck. Then he slid his hands around her waist and drew her close, close enough to touch his lips to her earlobe, her cheek, her nose, her forehead. "I don't need an affidavit, or a prenuptial, or anything else. I want you to share my life. All of it. We'll use the money to honor God."

"I like that," she said shyly. "I love you, Ben."

"I love you, Jayne."

They sealed their love with a kiss.

"I finally understand why you chose the pseudonym David."

"King David. The man God loved. The man who, for all his faults, loved God with his whole heart. 'My protection and success come from God alone,'" Ben recited.

"That's in the front of all your books." She smiled as she let her fingertip graze his beloved cheek. "That's why they're so successful. That and your talent."

"Thank you." He kissed her cheek. "I don't keep the money from the books, Jayne. It goes to Restart. I should have told you that, too."

"Then you gave me the loan?" she asked, frowning. "Because you felt sorry for me."

"No way, lady. I do not feel sorry for you. There is nothing to feel sorry about. You are the strongest woman I've ever known. You're brave and loving and honest and determined. All the things I most admire."

"You forgot stubborn." She laughed at his expression. "I do love you, Ben Cummings. I love David Bentley, too. But Ben's my favorite."

"Good to know." He kissed her nose.

"About that loan—"

"Truly, Jayne, all I did was to give you the papers and approve the other board members' decision to lend to you. You gained the loan on your own merits."

"Thank you for telling me that."

"I have lots of things to tell you. But I can't do it right now. I have to face those reporters." He kissed her once more, quickly, before easing her out of his arms. "I think you should go home, so you're out of the fray."

"No way." Confident of her love and of the Father's love

that had brought them together and would see them through their future, she placed her hand in his. "No more outsider, remember? We're in this together."

"Jayne, darling, you have no idea what reporters are like." He cupped her face in his palms, stared into her eyes. "Nothing in your life will be sacred from now on."

"They can't touch me, Ben. Not as long as you love me. Not as long as our protection and success come from God alone," she reminded.

"That's another reason I love you." Ben kissed her, folded her hand in his and grabbed the doorknob. "Ready?"

Jayne squeezed her eyes closed, whispered a prayer then smiled at him.

"Ready."

Together they stepped forward to face their future.

Epilogue

Very early Easter morning, Ben picked up Jayne at the condo. Together they waited in the darkness of his beautifully landscaped yard and watched the pink gold of sunrise creep across the clear cerulean sky.

"I'm sorry your parents aren't here to share our happiness, my darling," Ben whispered, his strong arms around her, his lips pressed against her ear.

"They are. All Heaven is celebrating, Ben." Jayne turned in his embrace, so she was facing him. "That's what Granny Em said. And Emma is never wrong."

"Look."

Jayne turned to see the big yellow sun crawl over the horizon, splashing the earth with its warmth. When it was fully visible, she looked at Ben.

"He is risen."

"He is risen indeed," he responded in the age-old greeting.

"I'm so glad we got everything out in the open last night."

"Me, too, though it was wild for a few minutes. I'm guessing we'll be under the spotlight for a while," Ben said. "Until another, better story comes along to replace David Bentley."

"Or until your next book. But I'm okay with that." She grinned.

"Good. The reporters were actually pretty fair about giving us some space today. Having Jerry there was a help." Ben shook his head. "But tomorrow, don't be surprised to find them lurking in Rose's Roses or your new landscaping site."

"Mmm, free publicity." Jayne laughed at his dour glance. "With God's help, we'll get through it."

She checked her watch and sighed. "The flowers," she said quietly.

Ben nodded, drove them both to Rose's Roses, where they loaded his car with fragrant arrangements and vases.

"And two Easter lilies, in pots." Jayne giggled as she set them on the floor. "You looked so wary that day."

"You looked mad."

"We were both dumb." Jayne placed big pastel bows in front of the little evergreens Ben had set in front of the church on that very first day they'd met. Then she helped him arrange the flowers around the set which the committee had put together the night before. When it was finished, she stood back, amazed. "It looks just like what I've always imagined the garden of Jesus's tomb would look like," she whispered. "The setting for God's biggest gift to us."

Ben's hand slid into hers as they remembered the sacrifice of their Lord. When Jayne moved, Ben drew her back.

"Jayne Rose," he murmured, "I love you very much. Will you please marry me?" In the palm of his hand nestled a black velvet box.

The fragrance of the Easter lilies mixed with hyacinths and jonquils filled the sanctuary and rose to the rafters. Jayne looked from the box to his face and saw love shining there, for her. A smile stretched across her face and she couldn't have stopped it if she'd wanted.

"I love you, too, Ben Cummings. Yes, I will marry you."

He kissed her thoroughly then opened the box and slid a beautiful ring onto her finger.

"It's a rose," she whispered, studying the setting for the yellow diamond.

"A desert rose," he agreed. "For *my* desert rose."

Jayne had no words. But it turned out she didn't need them as the choir, perfectly in pitch and four-part harmony, broke into the "Hallelujah Chorus."

* * * * *

Dear Reader,

Hello! I'm so glad you decided to join me for this mini visit to Palm Springs. It's a place I've especially enjoyed as a retreat, a vacation spot and a place of always changing beauty. *Desert Rose* touches on a topic so many of us battle—that of fear, which generates worry. As Jayne and Ben discovered, fears and worries happen because we lack trust in our precious heavenly Father. Few characters of the Bible had more reason to worry than David, yet no matter how desperate his plea, he always remembered who God was and that his deliverance came from the One who knew his heart.

As you celebrate Easter, I pray you'll find deep peace, a fount of great joy and trust in the perfect love of the one who gave his life for us, knowing that he will always be there to hear our cries and to wipe our tears.

Blessings to you, dear friends.

QUESTIONS FOR DISCUSSION

1. King David is a major figure in Biblical history. Discuss his life and the mistakes he made both before he was king and during his reign.

2. In the story, Jayne carries a lot of past baggage that has made her wary of trusting anyone, especially God. Consider issues in your own past and how they continue to affect your life today. What is holding you back from being free of your past?

3. Define fear. Was Jayne's fear of surgery really a lack of trust? Suggest ways we can identify fears in our own lives which hold us back from fully experiencing God's care for us.

4. Ben said he'd prayed many times for a woman to love him for himself. Are such prayers Biblical? Discuss ways we can open ourselves to love in our lives and ways we can safeguard our hearts against love that isn't genuine.

5. Easter was the time when Emma and Jayne remembered death. But at the end of the book it also becomes a time of joy and new life. Suggest ways we as Christians can share the hope that Easter is meant to give.

BLUEGRASS EASTER

Allie Pleiter

For knitters everywhere who know it's about so much more than just the yarn and needles.

Acknowledgments

I could not have crafted this story without the help of the wonderful people at Esther's Place Fiber Arts Studio. Natasha and Donna Lehrer shared their insights, anecdotes, facts and faith in a way that made this story a special gift for me as both a writer and a knitter.

Be shepherds of God's flock that is under your care,
serving as overseers—not because you must, but
because you are willing, as God wants you to be.
—*1 Peter* 5:2

Chapter One

Two o'clock in the afternoon was one of Audrey Lupine's favorite times in the library. Adults only. The little children—staples of any weekday library crowd—had gone home for naps and the rambunctious teen after-school crowd had yet to arrive. She could actually manage a cup of tea at her reference desk this time of day. Not exactly the English high tea, but close enough. She was just inhaling the luxurious aroma, browsing through a textbook, when a blond head bobbed up to the desk.

"How old are *you?*" A round pink face framed in layers of wavy blond hair topped the desk edge. A set of elbows parked themselves just under the face.

"Pardon?"

"The lady at my old library—" she mispronounced the word in a way other people might find adorable "—was really old."

Audrey was pretty sure twenty-nine was not anywhere in the neighborhood of "old." What parent had taught—or more precisely forgotten to teach—this little girl to mind her manners? "I guarantee you I am not 'really old.' But even if I were, that's not a nice question to ask."

The girl's blond brows scrunched together over pale blue eyes. "Why not?" Her head disappeared below the desk only to bob up again, this time with a yellow backpack. "You can ask *me* how old *I* am." She granted it like the greatest of favors. A magnanimous grade school gesture. "Go ahead, ask."

"I won't." I'm debating with a second grader. Worse, I seem to be debating decorum with someone under four feet tall. Audrey closed the textbook with what she hoped was a "this conversation is now over" thump.

No such thing. "I'm seven and three-quarters. Dad says I'm seven and thirty, but I'm not sure what that means." The head bobbed up and down now, alternating heights, as if standing on...

Oh, no. "You're not standing on your books, are you, young lady?"

Blink. Pause. "Nope." The head bobbed back down again, and Audrey heard suspicious scrambling. Audrey counted to ten and reminded herself that even precocious second graders grew up to read books. As for the remark about "seven and thirty," Audrey agreed with "Dad" one hundred percent. Now if only Dad would show.

"So how old *are* you?"

"Did your daddy ever tell you some questions aren't nice to ask? Especially to ladies?" Wouldn't Gran have had a field day with this little one? Gran had loved the wild things little kids said, just ate remarks like this up like candy. Despite her years in the library, Audrey hadn't inherited Gran's tolerance for youthful antics.

"Mom was thirty-one. She told everyone."

Audrey was just about to take this little girl to task for blurting out her mama's age when it hit her. She'd said "was." As in the past tense of *is*. As in *is no longer*. Normally she wasn't much for insight where young ones were concerned, but Audrey sensed a need to extend a little grace here. Even if the little girl was using books for steps and asked a woman's age. Twice. Audrey pushed back her chair and came around to the front of the desk. "I think thirty-one is a nice age."

She was dressed in the blinding style of a little girl who picked out her own clothes. Pink socks with green tights under a purple skirt with a blue sweater bearing red ruffles. A riot of color to match her outrageous personality. Uneven pigtails only rounded out the effect. She tucked her hands behind her, bouncing back against the desk in a fidgety rhythm. "I think angels don't get an age. What do you think?"

You could drive a truck through the subtext on that one. Angels. Mama was in Heaven, maybe? Audrey's heart melted. A little girl who'd lost her mama was just about the saddest thing ever.

"Maybe," Audrey said, squatting down to the little girl's height and trying desperately to ignore the smudgy footprint that graced the stack of early-reader books, "angels get whatever age they want. You know, get to pick one. That'd be fun, don't you think?" She scooped up the books as casually as she could manage. "I'd pick twelve, personally."

The child's face scrunched up in puzzlement. "Twelve?" She balked, obviously thinking it a pretty poor choice. "Why twelve?"

"I remember being really happy when I was twelve. My grandma taught me to knit when I spent the summer at her house. She lived on a lake and I got to go swimming a lot. It was a good year." She paused for a moment before gently asking, "So, Miss Seven and Three-Quarters, do you have another name I could use?"

"Me? I'm Lilly."

"That's a nice name. Who brought you here today, Lilly?"

"Oh, Daddy," she said as if it were obvious and began bouncing herself off the desk front again. The hollow, echoing thump reverberated through the library's quiet.

"Um," Audrey said, taking one of Lilly's hands to pull her off the desk and stop the percussive thuds, "do you think Daddy might be wondering where you are?"

"Oh, no," she replied, now inspecting the cup of pencils poised for patrons' convenience at the edge of the desk. "He knows we're at the library."

Audrey caught the cup of pencils just as it tipped over the edge. "Do you think Daddy might be wondering *where* in the library you've gone off to? I wouldn't want him to worry." Now this wasn't a genuine question. Even a seven-and-three-quarter-year-old could stand in the center of the Middleburg public library and see every corner from one spot. This library wasn't big enough to misplace anyone.

Lilly, of course, had a solution for this, and simply yelled "Da-a-a-d-d-y!" without the slightest hesitation.

While earsplitting and highly inappropriate, it was effective. Before the second syllable—well, actually, Lilly's rendition somehow had four syllables—a man with matching blond hair came darting out of the nonfiction stacks with a duly mortified look on his face.

"Lilly, I *asked* you to stay by Daddy while he found his books." He gave Audrey what she called "the parent look," the regretful shrug parents gave any member of the library staff when their unattended children misbehaved. Only this time, "the parent look" was replaced by an equally mortified look of recognition. "Oh, my, you're our neighbor, aren't you?" He looked down at Lilly. "What do you know, Lilly. We live next to the librarian."

Audrey should have recognized him. Lilly and her father were the ones who just bought the old farmhouse next to her place. She'd seen him from a distance, waved hello from the driveway, but hadn't yet talked up close.

Lilly evidently wasn't too impressed. "She wouldn't tell me how old she is."

Daddy offered a guilty smile while snatching Lilly up by the elbow. "We live next to the smart, kind librarian who's about to get an apology from you."

Lilly mumbled an obedient if not heartfelt "Sorry," her small chin jutting out with pint-size authority.

Dad then offered his hand. "Paul. Paul Sycamore. Sorry about Lilly's questions. She's…um…fascinated with women's ages lately." He hoisted a backpack over one shoulder and tucked one hand into the pocket of his brown corduroy pants. With the T-shirt and plaid flannel shirt, he had the look of an overgrown college student. A scruffy brand of charm but with an intellectual edge. Definitely not the average Middleburg guy. He leaned in a bit and lowered his voice. "We lost her mom—my wife—a while ago and it's just this thing she seems to do. I'm sorry if she wasn't nice about it." He said it with a resigned normalcy—as if he spent every day surrounded by such a sad truth—and it made Audrey's throat tighten up.

"I *was* nice," Lilly disputed.

"Actually, she was," Audrey offered, caught up in a sudden sympathy for the young widower. He looked like a nice guy, he really did. He had an inexplicable slowness about him that looked a bit like resignation. As if he'd long given up being startled by anything. Which was an awful lot of inferences to make about someone from such a casual meeting, but Audrey was surprised by the strength of the impression, "Lilly is direct, I'll grant you," she explained, "but she was nice. Well, nice-ish. For almost eight, I suppose."

"We don't even have a library card yet. Things have been a bit hectic, getting Lilly settled in school and all."

Gran would have had her hide for not having gone over to the new neighbor with a good Kentucky welcome. And she would have, if the ewes hadn't been so needy this week. She'd been out in the barn twice a night for "the girls," who seemed oddly agitated by the February weather. Still, she should have been able to make it over with some cookies from Dinah Rollings's bakery, if not something home-baked. Audrey turned her attention to Lilly. "Are you going to King's Christian Academy? I think I saw you last week when I brought some books over. Are you in Ms. Madison's class?"

"Yup. I can read chapter books already." She pointed to the stack of books she'd abused in front of Audrey's desk.

"All the more reason to have a library card. But you have to promise, no more standing on books."

Mr. Sycamore looked shocked. "You stood on the books? She knows better, really." He eyed his daughter. "Keep that up and they may not give you a library card."

"They have to." Lilly planted her hands on her hips. The girl had no shortage of attitude, that was certain.

"Actually," Audrey said, peering over her glasses, "we don't."

Lilly looked shocked.

"But on the promise that you'll do no such thing again, I'll give you a card."

The registration process provided Audrey with a host of information about her new neighbor. He'd moved from Pennsylvania, Lilly was his only child, and most interesting of all—he was a veterinarian. Very handy neighbor for a librarian with the world's smallest sheep farm. Four sheep wasn't really a farm, even though she called it that.

Dr. Sycamore was quick to point out, however, that he was taking a break from his veterinary practice. "On sabbatical," he called it.

"Further study?" Audrey asked. That's what people took sabbaticals for, wasn't it?

"Actually," Lilly's father said a bit shyly, "to write. I'm working on a novel. I've been saying I'd write one for years." His voice got the sad tinge again, and she noticed Lilly looked down and stubbed her foot against the base of the desk.

"I have to say, I admire your effort. I meet lots of people who say they want to write a book, but you're the first person I've met who's actually followed through on that." She tried to make her voice sound as encouraging as possible. "What kind of book?"

"Spy novel, actually. Having to do with horse training, breeding, the international racing circuit, that sort of thing."

She'd expected something closer to *All Creatures Great and Small*. Or a veterinary topic. "Really?" Spy novel? It sounded downright exotic.

"I had a fair number of equine patients back in Pennsylvania, and there's certainly no lack of research material here."

"Well, you'll find lots of folks willing to talk horses here," Audrey said. "We've even got breeders from Dubai down the pike. Start with Howard Epson, our mayor. He's more of a hobby breeder, but Howard knows everyone and I know he'd be happy to introduce you around."

"I've met Howard." Dr. Sycamore shifted his backpack and pushed a strand of wavy blond hair off his forehead. "He came over the day after we moved in. It was kind of nice, actually. Never expected to have the mayor come out and give me an official welcome."

That sounded like Howard. He liked to be the first at anything, and he definitely liked to be official.

"You have lambs." Lilly pointed at her. "I saw them."

"I have *ewes*. Lady sheep are called ewes. Four of them. But I bred one of them last fall, so I will have a lamb or two soon."

"Your sheep are funny. They stare at me. They're furry. And stinky."

Dr. Sycamore rolled his eyes. "Lilly, you know better than that. You've come to work enough times with me to know that all animals smell a bit. Mrs.—" he peered down to look at the nameplate on Audrey's desk "—Lupine's sheep look pretty clean to me. They're friendly. And they don't smell bad, they just smell like sheep."

Lilly wasn't changing her opinion. "They're really furry."

"Technically," Audrey said as she finished typing up the Sycamores' library card, "they're really *fleecy*. But not for long. My sheep are getting haircuts on Friday afternoon. I spin their fleece into yarn for my knitting, you know." She handed the card to the father. "And it's *Ms.* Lupine."

"Your sheep are getting haircuts?" Evidently Lilly found the idea startling.

It must have been the girl's adorably baffled expression. There simply wasn't another explanation for why Audrey blurted out, "They are. Want to come watch?"

Chapter Two

Paul pulled his green Mustang into the parking lot at King's Christian Academy and walked toward Ms. Madison's class. The children were out at recess, enjoying a swatch of February sunshine.

For all the highly pleasant surroundings—KCA was about as picturesque a school as anyone could imagine—Paul still felt unready for yet another parent-teacher conference. They were so much harder without Caroline. Yes, her cancer kept her from most school events toward the end, but Caroline *absent* wasn't ever the same thing as Caroline *gone*. He could always go and talk things over with her. Even at the end when she was barely awake an hour in a day, he'd go into her room and talk himself through the household issues. Now, especially with Lilly acting up so much lately, he felt truly alone. Almost two years alone—he thought he'd be more used to it by now.

Any number of household things still baffled him. Christmas decorations. Brownie Scout merit badges. Tights. He'd barely figured out how to make Lilly's pigtails last month. Paul was pretty sure he was going to have to ask some horse groomer to show him how to braid soon.

"I'm glad you could come," greeted Ms. Madison. She looked too calm as she motioned to the only two full-size chairs in the cheerfully decorated room.

"What's wrong?" Paul tried to sound less panicked than he felt. Maybe it was unreasonable to expect Lilly to handle a move well on top of all life had thrown at her. He was only just getting a hold on his own life.

"Oh, there's nothing wrong, actually. I think Lilly's doing well."

That sounded qualified to Paul, as if she'd hadn't said the "considering" she was obviously thinking. "She's acting up a bit at home," he admitted. Well, maybe not. What exactly was normal was for kids that age? Paul knew more about what to expect from a calf than a little girl. The strategies didn't exactly translate. "She keeps asking women their age. You can imagine how *that* goes over."

Ms. Madison laughed. "Seems like a healthy impulse to me. She's trying to figure out if everything that's happened to her is normal or unusual. She's very bright, but I gather you knew that."

Do very bright girls cut open their stuffed animals to "look inside?" Do they insist on blue sweaters four days in a row? Paul knew some really smart students in vet school who did weird things, but he wasn't sure Lilly's latest antics were a function of intellect. Then again, he did put a dozen frogs in his mama's freezer just to see if they'd survive when he was Lilly's age. "I suppose," he offered, thinking a neutral answer the wisest option at the moment.

"Actually, it's Lilly's ability to process what's around her that is the reason I wanted to talk to you, Dr. Sycamore."

"Paul," he corrected. He wasn't feeling much like Dr. Sycamore these days.

"Paul, the truth is that Lent and Easter are coming. As we

study the Easter story, I want to be sensitive to Lilly. We talk about death and resurrection. I think it's still rather fresh for her, so I'm hoping to do a little planning with you to make sure she gets as much of a positive experience from this as she can."

How exactly do you make a giant, gaping wound a "positive" experience? Paul was pretty much counting on merely surviving Easter, not gaining anything from it. Caroline had died on February 26, so his first Easter without her was pretty much a blur of pain and grief. Last year's wasn't much better. Maybe it was time he improved on that for Lilly's sake. "I hadn't really thought about it."

"I think you should ask her what she knows about Easter, ask about where she thinks her mother is now, questions like that. Nothing too pointed, just some casual questions here and there so we can give her some extra care where she needs it."

"I think I can do that. I'd planned to take her out to lunch today, maybe I'll throw in a question or two." Grade-school life-and-death theology over grilled cheese? He'd survived worse.

Lilly arranged the four triangles of her sandwich in two rows, points up, the way she'd started doing lately. "Why up?" Paul asked.

"So Mom can see them." Lilly answered as if it were an everyday fact of life. "They're waving at her."

The thought stuck in Paul's throat for a raw moment. "Greetings from Lilly's grilled-cheese sandwich, huh?" he managed almost casually.

"Yep. I got the idea from the trees. Ms. Madison says the trees clap their hands to God, so I figure my things can wave to Mom."

Paul silently wondered if perhaps Lilly's grasp of life-and-death theology wasn't stronger than his own. With a smirk, he took his Reuben sandwich and tried to make the half rounds of rye wave to Heaven.

They fell over, spilling out sauerkraut, and making Lilly giggle. "Yours *can't,* Dad."

"I guess not. I bet Mom thinks it's as funny as you do."

"Yep."

Gina Deacon, the friendly woman who owned the diner, came over with two new glasses of chocolate milk. "Gotta say," the big woman said, smiling, "I ain't had a guy your size drink this stuff in years."

Paul was so used to people thinking it odd that he drank chocolate milk with Lilly that it took him a second or two to realize she was paying him a compliment.

"Dad says life's too short to drink white milk," Lilly pronounced.

Gina fairly beamed at Lilly. "Well, three cheers for your Dad, honey. World needs more people like you, if you ask me. Paul, you and Lilly are welcome here anytime." She winked. "This round's on the house. 'Cuz, as I've just learned, life's too short not to drink *free* chocolate milk."

For all his angst, Paul really *did* feel welcome here. Gina had asked—and remembered—his name from his second visit. She was always so warm and cheery toward him. People back in Pennsylvania didn't know what to say to him after Caroline died, so they often just nodded and didn't say much of anything. Anyone but his best friends seemed afraid to have too long a conversation with him, fearing it would venture into sad topics. In their defense, Paul suspected he wasn't the best of company. Even Lilly had called him "a sourpuss" frequently in the months after Caroline was gone. There was something healing in being treated like a normal person, not the epicenter of tragedy.

"And you, Miss Lilly, may I say I do like what you do with a grilled cheese?" She nodded toward the three remaining upright triangles of sandwich. "Looks so much fancier that way."

Lilly beamed. "It's waving." Paul couldn't decide if he was sad or grateful Lilly hadn't offered the full explanation. He was living in that odd gap of not knowing who knew he was widowed and who didn't yet know.

Gina peered at it, then simply shrugged her shoulders and waved back. "I suppose it is. You're one happy girl, Lilly. Hey, soon you'll be one happy Easter Lilly. Imagine that!" she said as she went back toward the kitchen.

Well, now, this is what happened when you prayed for God to hand you the right opening to a difficult conversation. "Yep, Lilly, Easter's coming soon." For lack of a better segue he tried, "What *do* you think of that?"

"I get chocolate, right?"

Paul gulped at the thought of assembling an Easter basket. Like much of last year's Easter celebrations, baskets hadn't happened. "Yes, you'll get Easter candy. But what do you know about the Easter story? You know, the one in the Bible. Have they talked about it in school at all?"

"Jesus and the empty tomb."

"That's the one."

Lilly's face scrunched up in thought, and Paul waited patiently for the words to surface. "Mom said Jesus was her friend."

Caroline used that term all the time. She tried mightily to impress upon Lilly that Jesus should be her friend, too. She had always said watching her daughter's faith come to maturity would be one of the things she'd miss most. Well, that and the big wedding. Caroline loved weddings. Their own, not a week after Paul graduated from veterinary school, was a full-blown extravaganza. "It's true. Mom and Jesus were good friends."

"Now they're 'specially good friends, don't you think? Jesus got to go to Heaven at the end of Easter. And Mom's there, so they're near each other."

Paul fought the king-size lump in his throat. He couldn't manage much more than "Yep."

"I like being near friends."

"Do you miss your friends from Pennsylvania? We could call some of them."

"I got new friends here, too."

"And we're nearer to Grandma and Grandpa now, so we get to see them more, too."

Lilly selected a triangle from her plate and popped too much of it in her mouth. Her cheeks puffed out like a chipmunk's, and she didn't bother to swallow before saying, "I like it here."

A week ago Paul had to fake his agreement. Now he really meant it when he said, "You know, I do, too."

A million tiny healings, the grief counselor had said.

Chapter Three

He's *huge.*

That was the only thought Audrey had about the new shearer who pulled up in his truck Friday afternoon and unloaded his gear. Well, of course he has to be, lugging sheep around all day, but he looked huge and rather grumpy. Suddenly she wasn't sure she'd found the right man for the job, especially after how rough least year's shearer had been. No brute was going to get near her "girls" with a power tool!

Lilly and Paul had come over half an hour ago, so that Lilly could get to meet Martha, Mary, Ruth and Esther before and after their "haircuts." The quartet of ewes, whom Audrey always thought of as "the girls," were big lumbering things with all the fleece. They looked portly, a bit dirty and not at all like the dainty lambs they still were in Audrey's mind. She was looking forward to the surprise Lilly would get when they were restored to their gleaming white, much skinnier selves. The whole process struck Audrey as every woman's fantasy—shedding the older, tubbier self for the sleek, fresh person you were underneath all along.

Audrey was most anxious for Martha, the sheep who had

been bred, to get her fleece off. Every very pregnant woman Audrey had ever known had looked so uncomfortable, lumbering about just like the ewes, that Audrey was looking forward to relieving Martha of the cumbersome wool.

Dr. Sycamore was inspecting each of the sheep, evidently unable to drop his vet's curiosity in the face of such friendly animals. He'd been slightly friendlier in the few days since their encounter in the library, but that still didn't mean she knew him well enough to be able to judge when to ask ve questions and when such questions would be an imposition And really, small talk with handsome men had never been strength. Audrey managed facts and information easily. Relationships? Well, that was another story.

Lilly laughed when Martha was upended for shearing. I was funny—the sheep were essentially sat on their back sides, front hooves dangling awkwardly in the air, hind leg spread out in front of them, like great furry trolls sitting wit their bellies to the world. Up on their feet, they had a socia air about them—talkative, fidgeting, slightly nervous Upended, they sat drowsily and looked, well, not too brigh "They'll stay calmer that way," George the Enormou Shearer explained to Lilly when she asked why they couldn' stand up for the process. "They know I'm in control, and won't hurt 'em."

Lilly jumped when George turned on the shears—the were loud, sounding more like little hedge trimmers tha anything one would see in a barbershop. George started o one shoulder, and the white of Martha's undercoat appeare like the pith of an orange peel.

"Oooo," Lilly said, pointing. "Daddy, look how pretty it underneath!"

"It is, isn't it?" Audrey said, squatting down to Lilly height. "They'll make such pretty yarn, won't they?"

"How do you knit *that?*" Lilly asked, as Martha's coat began to peel off as one great sheet of wool.

"Lots of things have to happen to it first before it becomes yarn. I'll show you if you like."

"Ms. Lupine has other things to do than spend her days doing arts and crafts with you, Lilly." Paul caught her gaze over Lilly's head, as if to say, "You don't really have to."

And normally, Audrey wouldn't have. Still, something irresistible about the girl's wonder tricked Audrey into such invitations. With Gran gone, Audrey had a sharper yearning to share all the things she loved about yarn and knitting with someone who didn't merely tolerate it as "Audrey's hobby." There was a perfect circle about it, passing things down to another generation just as it had been done to her. "No, really," she said, smiling at him. "I'd like it."

Just then Martha bleated and scampered her new, clean self upright.

"She's naked!" Lilly cried. Audrey had to admit, Martha did sort of look as if she was in the sheep version of underwear—all white and thin and a little startled. Her pregnant belly showed clearly now, and Audrey thought of the little white lamb that would grace her barn in the coming weeks.

"She'll be much more comfy now," George said, winking at Lilly. "It's always best for them to be shorn before lambing. Ms. Lupine's a good shepherdess. Next?"

"Esther," Audrey said, popping up to guide the next sheep over to George. Esther bleated what Audrey suspected was a "nice to meet you," and abruptly turned away.

"Oh, no you don't," George said, catching her by the ears, angling her back against his massive legs before flipping Esther as unceremoniously as he'd flipped Martha. He patted her all over, inspecting her fur. "Um, which one is this again?"

Dr. Sycamore got a funny look on his face and stood up.

He walked to the fence, turning away from her, as if he thought a woman with only four sheep ought to be able to tell them apart.

"That's Esther, of course."

"And you said Martha was lambing, right?"

"Yes. Martha is lambing."

George patted Esther's belly, looked up and smiled. "Well, so's Esther."

"No. Just Martha." Audrey stood up.

"You tell that to Esther."

Esther had not been bred. "How?" Audrey gulped.

George's smile grew wide and amused. "Well now, Ms. Lupine, when two sheep love each other very much…"

"Not *that* how." Audrey bobbed her head furiously in Lilly's direction. "Dusty was only allowed in the pen with Martha." Dr. Sycamore coughed. "We took precautions," she continued. "There was a fence between Dusty and the other ewes."

George laughed. "I like this Dusty fellow."

Well, it had been unrealistic, Audrey supposed, to have a ram and ewes near each other for several weeks and not expect some…courtship…to go on. Still, she was sure she'd controlled any wandering on Dusty's part. She'd never found him outside his assigned pen. Ever. "It's a surprise," she said carefully. "But with a little bit of research I can plan for two lambs."

"Three," George corrected. "Esther here's lookin' like she'll have twins."

"Three lambs." Audrey began pacing the pen, facing away from the two men, scrambling to get her thoughts together. Wait a minute. If Esther, then…

George's long whistle ground her panicked projections to a halt. "Ms. Lupine?"

Audrey turned slowly, feeling the air thin out around her. "What?"

"You got a right bargain. All four of your ewes are lambing. And from the looks of it, all but Martha here are having twins. Mr. Dusty has my respect."

It was not possible. This simply couldn't be happening. "But…but he never left his pen. The fence…"

Dr. Sycamore stuffed his hands in his pockets, shrugging his shoulders. Oh dear, he'd known somehow, hadn't he? That's where that funny look on his face came from. "Fences can be jumped," he said.

How dare he make light of this crisis? Seven lambs. She'd have more lambs than sheep. "How could this happen?"

George snorted. "I think we just went over that, ma'am."

"I mean, I planned this all out. I did the research. It's not like I didn't know what I was doing. I knew *exactly* what I was doing."

George actually winked, "So did Dusty." He *winked*. What did he know? He'd get paid for shearing four sheep, pack up his things and be on his merry way while Audrey was left to cope with a population explosion that never should have happened. One lamb was perfect. She knew there was a possibility of two lambs, and was ready for that. But seven? And they supposedly would all come at once? She'd be overwhelmed.

She'd have to resign her post as chair of the Easter Parade, that's what. Maybe go to part-time at the library. Life had exploded beyond her capabilities and she was just going to have to pull out.

Audrey had never resigned anything in her life. Audrey Lupine never quit anything, because that's not the kind of carefully considering woman she was. She was the high school valedictorian, she'd known library science would be her field since her first semester at college. She had perhaps been accused by friends once or twice of preferring the company of books to real people—especially men—but one look around the available Middleburg bachelor pool could explain that in seconds. Now her…yes it had to be said… handsome new neighbor had a front row seat to this whopping mistake.

Audrey never made mistakes. She planned her vacations a year in advance and considered it a personal failing if the library ever ran out of anything. Oh my, she'd have to tell everyone. Everyone would have to know her enormous miscalculation here. She grabbed the fence post for support, her knees suddenly threatening to give way.

"Seven!" Lilly pronounced, holding up as many fingers. "That's a whole lot of baby sheep."

Audrey hoped she managed a smile. "Sure is."

George, who evidently possessed the ability to take catastrophes in stride, fired up his shears and started on Esther as if he'd simply changed socks or chosen wheat bread instead of white. "They's all looking fine and healthy, so I don't think you'll have too many problems. These mamas know how to look after their own."

Audrey did not share his relaxed view. "I can't have eleven sheep. I'm not prepared for eleven sheep. There'll be extra feed and vet costs and I don't have enough barn space for that many sheep."

"You'll have so much yarn!" Lilly pronounced.

"It may not be that big a challenge," her father offered. He definitely was a doctor. He had one of those "let's all try to stay calm" voices all doctors learn to use. "You don't have to keep them after they're weaned. It'll just be a short-term thing."

Audrey noticed that while his tone was encouraging and supportive, he did not utter the magic words *I'll help*. And why would he? They barely knew each other; he'd made it quite clear he was on leave from his veterinary practice; and this really was her own problem. A consequence for insufficiently supervising Martha's fleecy courtship. Really, was it that horrible a thing to allow two sheep their privacy during such a thing?

Evidently it was, for now she was paying for it. Six times over.

Chapter Four

Well, it doesn't get more awkward than this, Paul thought to himself as everyone tried to remain calm and cheerful for the last two sheeps' shearing. Had he done the right thing by not saying what he thought the moment he'd seen the sheep up close? He didn't really have much sheep clientele back in Pennsylvania, and he wasn't her vet. It seemed wrong to interfere. Still, the way Audrey shot him looks after he made the mistake of admitting he suspected before George did, maybe he should have spoken up.

Lilly was blissfully unaware of the tension in the pen, inspecting the sheep fleece George laid out on a table in the barn, touching the new white fur of the shorn sheep and generally adoring the four ewes now that they were "going to be mamas." He was glad she'd revised her earlier "stinky" assessment of them, glad to see her having fun, but painfully aware of the lamb bomb that had just been dropped on poor Ms. Lupine. She really did look undone by the whole thing. He'd always thought farmers and livestock owners—or arts-and-crafts types in general, for that matter—to be a more flexible, easygoing sort. He felt the urge to help, to take that look of utter panic off her face, but couldn't say how she'd react if he did. Offer? Wait until asked? This is why he liked animals—they were so much less complicated than humans.

Finally, after the shearing had been completed and Lilly was persuaded to walk the path back up to their house, Paul could make a graceful exit. There must have been something better to say than, "Well, if you need anything…" but his neighbor looked close to hyperventilating and he wasn't good at this sort of thing.

After making dinner for Lilly, they read one of her library books together, and she settled down with her dolls and some animal toys on the living room rug while he stared at his computer laptop. He'd wanted to write a lot this evening, but he was mostly just staring at that little blinking cursor on his page that refused to turn itself into words. Lilly was arranging the animals and dolls into a farm, he noticed with a fair amount of amusement, with all the participants shouting excitement over the "seven baby lambs."

He'd bailed on the blank page and was making some after-dinner coffee when he spied Audrey Lupine marching across the yard toward his back door. He sighed, dumped two extra spoonfuls of ground coffee into the filter and opened the door before she even raised her hand to knock.

"You said, 'if there's anything I can do,'" she explained as she stepped in.

"Yes, I did. I just put some coffee on."

"I'm really a tea person, but, I suppose I could manage a cup."

He watched her eyes scan the sparse decor of his kitchen. All the doodads of a home—place mats, curtains and such—had been Caroline's forte. Paul's mom was going to come out from Louisville tomorrow to get a start on all that, but for now the house was spartan to say the least. "I've got cream and sugar if you like."

"Both, please."

He hadn't even gotten the sugar bowl out from the cabinet before she pronounced, "I think I should fire my vet. The breeder was on his recommendation. He should have seen the living arrangement I'd set up to keep Dusty confined to Martha wouldn't work. I wanted to know what you think, if that's not imposing."

Paul pinched the bridge of his nose. How many times had he, as the vet delivering the bad news, been yelled at, blamed, snubbed or worse? And half of those times it was for problems caused by inattentive owners, not him or even the animals themselves. "Sheep aren't my specialty, but I don't think it's an exact science. Animals are full of surprises. Upsets happen. I know it's not what you were after, but this isn't something to fire your vet over. Especially if he's given you good service with your ewes in the past. You need him now more than ever."

"But I was not in *any way* ready for all four ewes to lamb."

"Seems to me, Ms. Lupine, life has a funny way of not caring what we're ready for." He hadn't meant for that remark to be about Caroline and her death, but somehow they both connected those thoughts at the same time, and it made for an even more awkward silence.

"I'm sorry for your loss," she said quietly, all the fight deflated out of her. "And Lilly's."

"Who's here?" Lilly came trotting out of the living room, a plastic sheep in one hand and a doll in the other. "Oh, hi. How are the mama sheep?"

"Very comfortable now." He watched Audrey smile. "The stack of their wool is almost as tall as you."

"You'll have lots of yarn when the babies come," Lilly repeated.

"I'm not going to worry about that just yet." Ms. Lupine accepted her coffee. "I've got more important problems to solve first." She dumped a generous amount of both cream and sugar into her coffee and stirred. "Dr. Sycamore…"

"Paul," he corrected, especially not wanting to be Dr. Sycamore at the moment. Maybe even anymore.

"Paul," she said uncomfortably. "This whole business is upsetting to me. I'm not some sort of impulsive, irresponsible person. I think my plans through. I had good reason to breed only one ewe. I'm quite certain I can't manage eleven animals." She hadn't drunk her coffee yet; her hands still held the mug in a white-knuckle death grip. "I don't have the barn space or enough pasture or the time to cope with that many sheep. I can't bear the thought of selling off any of the girls, but I'm just not prepared to deal with all those lambs. It should never have happened. I'm mortified that it happened. Honestly, I'd never have tried to breed Martha if I'd have known."

She should have known, Paul thought to himself. Farm life just doesn't contain itself to neat, mathematical projections. Paul felt a hint of annoyance at the vet who'd allowed her to believe livestock were that predictable.

"You don't want the babies?" Lilly asked with sad alarm in her voice.

"It's complicated, Lilly," Paul interrupted, seeing the look on Ms. Lupine's face. "Lambs take a lot of work, and Ms. Lupine…"

"Audrey," she corrected.

"Audrey's just worried that they won't get the care they need. She's being a responsible animal owner, honey, and that's a good thing."

"How can sending the lambs away be good? You said you wanted a lamb." Lilly was holding the plastic sheep, the one she'd just been playing "mama lamb" with, which made it all worse. He did think Audrey was overreacting, but people overreact when they get broadsided—he knew that from personal experience.

"One lamb and seven lambs are very different things," Paul offered. He motioned for Lilly to come up and sit on his lap. "Do you remember when I told you we were moving?"

"Yep." She made the plastic sheep walk around the place mat in front of Paul's coffee.

"You told me it was the worst idea ever. That you didn't want to go away from our old house. Do you remember?"

"I was mad," Lilly said, making a frowning face.

"And we like it now, don't we? But it was such a big idea then, such a new change, that it felt awful. Miss Audrey's had a big change thrown at her today. You need to remember that and be nice."

Audrey didn't respond, and Paul knew what he ought to say. He knew what a good neighbor would say, what a good Christian man ought to say. It was just sticking in his mouth, festering with such resistance that he couldn't do it. He couldn't offer to help. He was here to get away from the vet business, to re-create himself the way he'd promised Caroline. His mind went to the last missionary he'd heard at church, who said that he told God he'd go anywhere but China.

So God sent him directly to China.

It was an amusing story then. It was like someone fastened a millstone around his neck now. One that had Paul Sycamore, Doctor of Veterinary Medicine, Anywhere But Sheep etched on it. "It might not be as bad as you think," he said weakly.

She got the librarian look in her eyes. "I am quite certain I cannot handle seven lambs in the short term nor can I handle a flock of eleven in the long run." She took a sip of her coffee, and he watched her eyes narrow. Somehow, it was clear what she was thinking; she was heaping a pile of scorn down on poor Dusty, who was just, well, doing what rams do.

"It's not anyone's fault, you know," he said, half to her because she was beating herself up something fierce and half in defense of Dusty's God-given procreative instincts. "Things just happen."

"You're not going to give me that bit about God not giving us more than we can handle, *are you?*" she asked.

They must learn that in librarian school. Technically, that was a question, but it was way closer to a threat. "No ma'am," he said quickly. "That one hadn't even entered my head." He was glad it was true, because she seemed to be the type of person who could pick up a lie from a mile away.

"Do you think *God* sent you all those sheep?" Lilly seemed to think this was a grand way to look at things. Paul tried to think of chores Lilly might need to do this very minute or an appropriate DVD to pop into the player *now.*

"I think," Audrey said, "that I'm living with the consequences of making a bad choice." She really did make it sound that dire.

"Oh," Lilly consoled, "*con-se-quen-ces.* I know about those." She pointed to a red chair in the corner of the kitchen. "That's my time-out chair. It's for *con-se-quen-ces.*" She was so serious, had such an intent look of commiseration on her face, that Paul couldn't hide his chuckle.

Audrey actually managed a tiny smirk. "I'd like to put our friend Dusty in that chair."

Lilly thought that was hysterical, and erupted into a flurry of giggles. "He's a sheep, silly. He can't have a time-out chair!"

The resulting laughter reminded Paul why Lilly was such a special gift. Even in the worst of predicaments, even when things were beyond hopeless at the hospital or the hospice center, Lilly's laugh could spill sunshine into a moment. Audrey finally let her snicker dissolve into a genuine laugh. Paul looked at the small red chair and pictured the robust ram—who he'd never even met—teetering on that tiny chair the way George had flipped the ewes to teeter on their round, fleecy backsides. It was a hysterical image, and made him laugh harder.

"I suppose I should talk to Dr. Vickers before I fire him," Audrey admitted. "See what he thinks ought to be done."

"The breeder who offered you Dusty may have people looking for lambs," Paul suggested as he finished off his coffee. "You could sell them once they're weaned and just keep the one or two you were looking for."

"That's true. Still, I'm in over my head." She gave out a sigh. "I might have to take a leave from the library or go to part-time. And quit the Easter Parade for sure. I could never do both."

Lilly's eyes went wide. "A parade?"

"I'm surprised they haven't talked to you about it at school. The school will have a float in it, I'm sure. Middleburg is going to have its first Easter Parade this year, and…until now…I've been in charge of it." She took another sip of coffee. "That'll have to change."

"A parade. I'll get to be in a parade!" Lilly squirmed off Paul's lap to march around the kitchen singing, "Parade, parade."

"Just wait until I break the news to Howard. He'll put *me* in a red chair in the corner."

Paul had only met Howard twice, but he was pretty sure Audrey was right.

Chapter Five

"You can't. You just can't." Audrey had expected Mayor Howard Epson to be shocked, annoyed even, but he seemed to take her resignation as a personal blow.

"Howard, believe me, this wasn't my idea," Audrey argued as they met at the church Saturday morning. "I've got to be realistic. I can't do it."

"They're lambs. This is a horse-breeding town. It can't be that hard to find someone to take care of that for you."

Audrey leveled her best serious look at the mayor. "Howard, you're asking me to hire out my sheep to someone else, to fix a problem I made, so I can take on a volunteer chairmanship of a holiday parade?" She didn't say "be serious," but she hoped her eyes sent the message. It's not as if she thought this resignation would go smoothly. Howard was legendary for his ability to talk people into things they'd never have offered. The man was a civic force of nature.

"I'm asking you to serve your community in a way that only you can. This is your moment, Audrey."

"I hardly think I'm the only person in Middleburg who can

do this." She tried a different tack. "Who were you going to ask if I said no?"

She knew the flaw in her thinking the minute the words left her mouth. It came to her the same instant Howard said, "I knew you wouldn't say no." Howard wasn't the kind of man who bothered with a Plan B.

Because neither was she. Audrey Lupine was the kind of person who got the job done. Responsible. Dependable. An excellent time manager. After all, she'd had sufficient time to play the leading role in dozens of community theater plays. She'd always kept herself busy, and never for want of available projects. Her single status—in a town decidedly lacking in other single people—gave folks the illusion she had loads of free time on her hands. It wasn't true. Audrey suspected she didn't have any more hours in her day that God gave anyone else, she just managed those hours exceedingly well. Never overextended herself...until now. Now she'd have to convince Howard to let her off the hook—all because of something so trite-sounding as an "unexpected sheep incident." And that was how she'd come to think of it in her head. "The incident." A crime of passion—literally.

"I can't accept your resignation," Howard said formally.

It was all Audrey could do not to roll her eyes. "I don't have a choice here, Howard. Those lambs are coming whether I want them to or not."

"You can find a way to do both. You're a very smart woman, highly organized."

"Smart enough to know this won't work."

He looked at her, his face taking on those grandfatherly qualities she knew were his persuasive weapons but she couldn't seem to resist anyway. "Don't say no now. Think on it. Pray. Whip out those amazing planning skills of yours.

God's a mighty God, and I still believe you're the right gal for the job. You sleep on it and we'll talk again later."

"I…"

Howard was already gone, strutting off down the church hallway like a man who'd just turned back disaster. "Lord," she prayed aloud, "I'm going to need more guidance than that."

Unsure of what to do now, Audrey pushed open the doors that led into the empty church sanctuary. She needed guidance. Bucketfuls of it. *This was never supposed to happen, Lord. You value life. Every life. How do I value these lambs in the way You want when there's no way I can take care of them properly?* She looked up at the stained glass window to her right, seeing the familiar image of Jesus as the Good Shepherd, with a snowy lamb over his shoulders. He looked so calm. She'd loved the image before, now it seemed to mock her ineptitude.

Why'd You back me into this corner? What possible good could come out of a mistake like this? I know I should trust You, but it's no use trying to hide from You how panicked I am. I don't see the sense in this.

She didn't really expect the Good Shepherd Jesus to offer up wise counsel, but it would have been so nice if He did. As it was, she left the sanctuary with her thoughts still in tangles.

"I told you Howard wouldn't take no for an answer," Emily Sorrent said as she concentrated on her needles when Audrey met her in the town bakery that afternoon. Emily's baby girl was due in June and Audrey was teaching her to knit pink booties. "Oh, I dropped another stitch. How do I fix this again?" Audrey took the needles from Emily, admiring again the yarn's exquisite softness and "aww"-producing pink hue. Even with the smattering of new-knitter mistakes, the booties were adorable. She worked the wayward stitch back into place as she bemoaned her fruitless conversation with Howard. "I can't believe I backed down and said I'd think about it. I need to be off that project. I should have just marched down that hall after him and made him let me off." She handed the restored project back to Emily and took up her own project, a sweater for Emily's baby girl out of the same delectable pink yarn. She was so glad that Emily had asked for knitting lessons, and that together they were partnering to make the baby a matched set. It felt like loving this little girl into the world one stitch at a time.

"You'd be the first," Emily chuckled. "No one changes that man's mind." Emily started up knitting again. "Are you really having seven lambs? And you didn't know?"

Only twenty-four hours, and word had spread. It was making Audrey nuts to have to admit her ignorance to everyone in Middleburg. Lots of shepherds never know which of their ewes are lambing until they're shorn. She just never wanted to be "lots of shepherds." While Audrey understood that Dusty's adventures made for a highly amusing tale, she felt like all the fun was at her expense. The worst practical joke ever, with live, four-legged consequences. The word made her think of the equally amusing bit with Lilly and the red chair, and she told Emily the story.

"Paul seems really nice. Gil likes him." Gil, Emily's husband, wasn't exactly the welcoming type, so that earned Paul high marks from Audrey. "Gil told me he's joined the men's Bible study at church. It's so sad to see an adorable little girl without her mother."

Audrey thought of Lilly's great, round eyes, imagining tears flowing out of them instead of the sparkles she always saw. Little ones shouldn't be taken from their mamas. Not even sheep mamas.

"I can't sell them. The lambs, I mean. I'd have to sell the

ewes with their lambs so they wouldn't be separated, and I couldn't bear to lose the girls."

Emily put down her knitting. "Audrey, you're the sweetest person I know, and I adore you, but I'm sorry, honey—it has to be said. These are *sheep* we're talking about. Farm animals. I'm not even sure they'd know if you separated them."

"*I'd* know."

"You said it yourself. You don't have what you need to take care of all those sheep. What are you going to do?"

"I don't know. I'm stumped."

Dinah Rollings, owner of the bakery, and the only person Audrey had never been able to teach knitting—mostly because Dinah never sat down for more than ten seconds at a time—sauntered over to the little bistro table where the tea-and-knitting session was taking place. She'd been popping in and out of the conversation while tending to the bakery. "Maybe you don't *have* to know just yet." Dinah hooked a chair with her foot and pulled it over to sit on it backward as it faced the table. "Oh, Audrey, adorable just does not even begin to cover it. I don't even like pink and I can't take my eyes off those itty-bitty little booties."

"You just work your wonders with frosting, that's all," Audrey offered.

"How are the girls holding up?" Audrey loved that Dinah had taken to calling her flock "the girls," as well. "Ready for the Seven Wooly Wonders of Audrey's World?"

"The Seven Wooly *Worries* of Audrey's World, more like. My vet confirmed it—three of the girls *are* having twins. Come to think of it, the only one not having twins is the one who was *supposed* to be pregnant in the first place."

Dinah fingered the tiny ruffles that formed the bottom edge of the baby sweater. "Does make you wonder what God's up to, don't it?"

"This is my mistake, not an act of God. My oversight. My stupidity."

"You didn't know Dusty had jumped the fence? Didn't you find him in the other pen with the other ewes?" Dinah leaned her elbows on the chair back, hungry for a juicy story.

"The sneaky little fellow jumped back over, it seems. I mean, really. You just don't count on that level of deceit in an animal."

"Obviously," Emily said, rolling her eyes, "you've never owned a cat." Audrey had forgotten that Emily's cat, Othello, had given her and Gil no end of trouble when Emily moved out to Gil's Homestretch Farm. Still, it was a long way from "mouse presented at bedside" to "six surprise mouths to feed."

"Good thing you've got a vet right next door, though. That's got to be a blessing." Dinah offered.

"You'd think," replied Audrey as she resumed knitting. "But he's 'on leave' from his vet practice. The only help he's offered so far is admitting he suspected the girls were pregnant when he saw their bellies and confirming my shearer's opinion. The moment he announced it. Really, how embarrassing is it to have a whopping slipup like this revealed to you in front of a *vet?* He's been very nice and all, but I'm sure he doesn't think too much of my animal husbandry."

"Wait a minute," Emily said. "You said even your own vet didn't know, right? What makes you think you'd have figured it out earlier if no one else could? You should cut yourself a little slack, Audrey. And Paul, too. Maybe he's just waiting for you to ask for help. You know, trying not to intrude. My doctor friend says she never offers advice until she's asked. He might be the same way."

"I sat in his kitchen hysterical over the whole thing. How much more direct do I need to be?"

Emily turned her needles, smiling at the satisfaction of

having completed another row. "This is a man we're talking about. The blunt instrument species."

"Speak for yourself," Dinah teased. "Cameron would have offered twelve times already to come in and draw you up an action plan with charts and tables." Dinah popped off the chair, her eyes growing wide. "In Paul Sycamore's kitchen, hmm?"

"Asking him if I should fire my vet, thank you very much."

"Well—" Dinah twirled a lock of her bright red hair "—you did say *husbandry.*" Her teasing look was replaced by one Audrey knew too well—the unmistakable expression of Dinah Rollings getting a wild idea. "Hey, wait a minute, that's it."

Emily and Audrey exchanged looks. "What?" they said with simultaneous displays of trepidation.

"Have Cameron do his chart thing. Paul's in the same church Bible study as Cameron, right? Why don't we have Cameron do his math projection thing to see what you'd really need to deal with keeping all the sheep? If he gets Paul's input, then you can sort of gauge how willing he'd be to help without actually asking. He's just helping Cameron help you, not helping you personally. It's kind of like baking a pie with someone else's crust."

Audrey furrowed her brow. Dinah's crazy baking metaphors were the stuff of Middleburg legend. "That makes no sense, you know that." She moved her gaze away from Dinah while she executed a complicated stitch. "I have lots of information. I've done my own 'chart thing' you know, I don't go into ventures unprepared."

Dinah shrugged. "Leave it to me. I got it covered."

Audrey leveled a glare. "No."

"What do you have to lose? You need help—you said so yourself. Why stop me from seeing if I can get the handsome vet next door to lend a hand? It's like God installed him right next door at just the right time, if you think about it. You know, there are no coincidences…"

"Only God-incidences," Emily said, right on cue, completing Dinah's favorite phrase for her. "Dinah, don't get all match-'em-up on her. He's a widower. He's still got healing to do."

That was a new one—Emily had a reputation as the community matchmaker, so this really was the pot calling the kettle black, to indulge Dinah's love of metaphors. "Okay, so I *have* thought about it," Emily admitted under Audrey's glare. "It's not like I said anything out loud."

"Emily…" In truth, Audrey was surprised Emily had held off this long. Which meant, hopefully, that she shared Audrey's reluctance to consider any kind of relationship with someone coming off such a huge wound as the loss of a wife. It was a bad idea, plain and simple.

"Well, don't tell me you haven't taken a good long look yourself. Handsome, professional, Godly, caring dad, twenty-five yards to the east—it is rather…"

"God-incidental," finished Dinah.

"…convenient," Emily continued.

"None of your business," Audrey declared, hoping that would be the end of it.

"Oh, honey, you should know better than to try an old chestnut like that. This is Middleburg, where everything is everybody's business."

Chapter Six

Pastor Anderson put one hand on Paul's shoulder Tuesday night at Bible study. "So, how did yesterday go?" Despite the fact that it felt like going too deep too fast, Paul had felt compelled to share with the men's Bible study that Monday marked the two-year anniversary of Caroline's death. Even though the church hosted three different men's Bible studies, he'd asked to join the Tuesday-night group with older men because half of them were widowers, too. It was a bit hard to swallow that these guys referred to themselves as "the old coots," so he decided to take up Cameron Rollings's title and dub himself a "young coot." At thirty-five, he was a "middle coot," but that didn't seem to roll off the tongue. His "not-so-young coot" status had become a running joke of sorts, and that helped to make him feel as if he belonged. He'd felt like a trespasser in his own world for so long lately.

How did yesterday go? He wasn't sure himself. It was a confusing tangle of mixed emotions. "Okay, I guess. Better than I expected, I suppose." He fingered the spot where the wedding ring used to sit, which he often found himself doing when he talked about Caroline. He'd taken the ring off his finger on the first anniversary of her death, and not a moment before. "I thought I'd feel bad about not being back in Pennsylvania at the cemetery, but it seemed like a bad idea to pull Lilly out of school when she'd just settled in. My parents offered to watch her, but I didn't want to be far from her yesterday."

"Did Lilly talk about her ma?" Vern Murphy, the oldest of the group, who should have long since retired from his job at Bishop Hardware but just couldn't stay away, leaned in to ask.

"She did. And we teared up a bit, both of us, at breakfast, but the rest of the day was just a sad sort of normal. Nothing major, actually." Paul shifted in his chair. "You expect the big stuff to hurt, but lots of times it's surprising little things that really do you in. I found Caroline's sock in a box of Lilly's summer clothes last week and I walked around clutching the thing, trying not to sob, for two hours."

"That's when you should call one of us," Pastor Dave said. "This is your hometown now, and we want to be there for you." He sounded sincere, but Paul couldn't help thinking Pastors were *supposed* to say those kinds of things.

"Involvement is part of small-town life." Howard Epson offered, sounding like the mayor he was. "We help you, and someday you'll get the chance to help us."

"Funny you should bring that up, Howard," Cameron said. "I got a little project I could use your help on, Paul."

Paul couldn't possibly imagine what kind of help he could be to a real-estate broker, especially when that broker fished a piece of paper out of his pocket and spread a series of charts out on the table between them. Then he saw one of the headings—Sheep Feed.

"I've been trying to help Audrey figure out what to do about her sheep," Cameron explained.

"Heard about that little surprise." Vern chuckled.

"Well, it's not so little to Audrey." Cameron came to her

defense. "You know her. She doesn't like things to get out of hand."

"Little late for that, ain't it?" Vern chuckled again, until Pastor Dave silenced him with a look.

Cameron leveled a businesslike gaze at Paul. "Audrey's done her research, and she's sure she can't keep a flock that large. She won't sell the babies without their mothers, and it's breaking her heart. I'm thinking there has to be a way, somehow, to manage it. I've done a bit of research myself, but I was hoping you could look over my numbers."

"Shepherd with a laptop," Howard quipped, squinting at the massive tables and spreadsheets Cameron had created.

"He's not so far off. I had several clients back East where the animals had GPS markers. And I'm betting most of you have seen the setups Gil Sorrent has out at Homestretch Farm." Paul ran his eyes down the chart dealing with square footage of barn space. "Gil's the man to look at this, not me."

"I had Gil look at it," Cameron replied. "He said it looked sound, but he only knew horses. It was Gil's idea, as a matter of fact, to ask you."

"Audrey's threatening to quit the Easter Parade over this," Howard warned in serious tones. "We've got to do all we can." Paul was just thinking he wasn't sure it was quite the crisis Howard indicated when the mayor pierced him with a glare. "If you can help, Middleburg needs you."

The fate of seven lambs did not spell Middleburg's doom, but you'd never have known it by the look on Howard's face. Cameron wasn't too far behind. "I could use your expertise. I mean, you're a vet and all. There must be something you can do to figure out a strategy."

"I'm here to write, not to practice." Paul thought he'd need to have a sign made and posted in his front yard at this point.

"No one's asking you to deliver the lambs," Howard said.

Yet, Paul thought to himself.

"Audrey has a vet already."

"Oh yeah, and you should have heard the two of them arguing at the hardware store yesterday," Vern interjected. "They were there to order some special feed, and somebody over in the garden section made some smart-aleck remark about a 'Ca-lamb-ity,' and Audrey let him have it." Vern broke into a snicker remembering the scene. "Ca-lamb-ity. Pretty funny when you think about it." Howard leveled a glare at Vern, whose chuckle dissolved into a poorly disguised cough. "Or not."

"Dr. Sycamore," Howard said, his gaze not lightening up much when it turned on Paul, "the fact is that we need you. I'd like to think that even though you're new here, you'll do anything you can to help out."

Now he was going to look like a selfish jerk if he didn't at least look over a couple of sheets of paper. Only somehow, Paul knew it wouldn't stop there. On some bleak level, he knew that with a single suggestion to improve even one figure on that spreadsheet, he'd set a process in motion that might very well end him up knee-deep in lamb muck. He started to pray, *Lord, deliver me from…*until he realized the unfortunate wording of that impulse.

Audrey kept wringing her hands as Paul stood dripping in her barn Thursday afternoon. "I really appreciate this," she said, for the fourth time. "Really. She doesn't look right and Dr. Vickers hasn't returned my call yet." Audrey hung her soaked raincoat on the peg by the barn door and motioned for Paul to do the same. He did, but not before he helped Lilly out of the adorable duck slicker she wore—complete with matching galoshes and umbrella. Decked out in yellow and orange with huge blue eyes, Lilly was about as cute as a kid can get in a rainstorm. "Those are some amazing boots there, Lilly."

"They're from my grandma. Is Ruth sick?"

"I don't really know. That's why I asked your dad to come over." She offered Paul another apologetic smile. "Thanks again."

He just nodded. She'd tried mightily not to call him since he'd helped Cameron with his charts. Cameron's inconclusive charts that said Audrey might just be able to support the full flock on her pastures with supplemental feeds, but at considerable supplemental expense. "A doable stretch," Cameron had said. Audrey did not do "a doable stretch" with anything. She hadn't called Paul when Dr. Vickers told her Mary's coughing wasn't anything to worry about. Or when Esther didn't eat enough. These ewes were driving her to an obsessive worry. She was two days late—not one, but two days late—on her report to the library board. She'd snapped at a volunteer page yesterday because she'd been up all night going over Cameron's tables again. It had made her run straight to the Internet and look up all the diseases poor nutrition can bring to lambing mothers. Not to mention the dozens of things that insufficiently balanced nutrition could do to helpless lambs.

Paul's visit had become a matter of survival. Doctor Vickers wouldn't come out, and Audrey couldn't sleep if she wasn't certain the girls were okay. Given the choice between annoying Paul and having a panic attack, Audrey opted to drag her neighbor out in the rain.

"Well," said Paul, picking up his veterinary kit and shaking the last of the rain out of his hair, "let's see what we've got."

Paul spent about ten minutes going over every inch of Ruth—some of which the ewe didn't mind, some of which she highly objected to—while Audrey tried not to hover. Lilly made that easy, because that child's curiosity pulled her into everything. Audrey was running out of ways to politely say "don't touch that," and "stay out of there" before the first five minutes were over.

"She's edgy," Paul said with a sigh that was just a bit too big, "but I have a feeling that's more to do with the storm than anything else."

"I rushed them into the barn. The book says they can't get wet."

"They shouldn't get *drenched*. There's a difference. She looks in fine shape. If you're following the percentages you gave Cameron for his tables, you're doing fine."

"I don't want any of them stressed."

"They look happy to me," Lilly said. "Which one's this?" She pointed to the largest of the sheep.

"That's Martha."

Lilly scrunched up her face. "How do you know?"

"There are twelve girls in your second-grade class. How does your dad pick you out of all the little girls?"

"That's silly. He knows me. And only half of us have yellow hair. All your sheep have the same hair color."

Paul hunched down next to Lilly. "Look at Martha. Her eyes are very big and her ears stick out flat most of the time." He pointed to Ruth. "Her face is wider, and her nose has that funny tilt to it."

Lilly pointed to Mary. "Her nose is pinkier."

"More pink," Paul corrected, laughing. Audrey couldn't help but notice the way his face changed when Lilly amused him. An unconscious flood of tenderness that his normally quiet expression couldn't contain. "Now you get it. Audrey knows her sheep the same way I know you."

The verse stating *He knows His sheep and His sheep know Him* ran unbidden through Audrey's thoughts.

Lilly turned to Audrey. "So you're like Grandma. Your sheep are going to have grandlambies."

Audrey was too charmed to be insulted. She opened her mouth to correct the very disconcerting thought of her being anyone's grand-anything, but shut it again.

"Not really," Paul said, looking appropriately embarrassed. "Look, Audrey, your sheep are fine. Unsettled by the weather, yes, but honestly, there's nothing here that leads me to believe you've got any reason to worry. Sheep have been lambing for centuries, most of them without the benefit of veterinary medicine. God knows what He's doing and creation knows the ropes." He slipped his stethoscope back into the bag. "Quite frankly, the person who looks in the worst shape in this barn is *you*. You've got to calm down or you'll never make it through this."

For a guy who said he didn't want to be involved, that was pretty well over the "butting in" line. Trouble was, Dr. Vickers gave her exactly the same speech the last time she called. "I'm worried about them," she offered, trying not to sound as defensive as she felt. "I can't seem to stop worrying about them."

"Do you pray for them?"

Audrey wasn't expecting that. "Well…"

"I would. Even Lilly knows God cares about the things we care about, and you really care about your sheep. You need a heaping dose of peace, and I don't know too many other ways to get it than praying."

Audrey realized, by the dark shadow that passed over his eyes, that he spoke from experience. And why wouldn't a man who needed to get himself and his daughter through the death of the woman they both loved know about needing "heaping doses of peace"? She suddenly felt foolish making such a fuss. About calling him out into a rainstorm just to calm her unreasonable nerves. "I'm sorry," she said.

"Don't be sorry," he said, "just be calmer."

Lilly tugged on Paul's sleeve. "She needs cocoa, Dad. I do, too."

Audrey raised an eyebrow. "I make Lilly cocoa when she needs to settle down," Paul explained. "It works." He shrugged.

The least she could do was make hot chocolate for these two. And, if she did say so herself, Audrey made a wickedly good cocoa. "I have a special recipe, you know," she declared. "People say I made the finest cocoa in the county."

"Nope," Lilly said. "Dad makes the best."

Audrey adopted a Texas-size drawl and planted her hands on her hips. "Them's fightin' words, young'un. Your daddy use whipped cream?"

Lilly planted tiny pink fists on tiny yellow hips. Calamity Jane in ducky boots. "Yep. Lots."

Audrey remembered some ice-cream toppings at the back of her spice drawer. "Sprinkles?"

Aha, superiority achieved. Lilly looked back at her dad as if to say, "you never told me we could put sprinkles on cocoa."

Now, Audrey was not normally a "sprinkles" kind of person. As a matter of fact, she couldn't remember why it was she even had the sprinkles in her kitchen in the first place. And she definitely didn't think of herself as the "good with kids" type, either. But the swell of satisfaction at besting Paul Sycamore in cocoa creation, the look of startled surprise in Lilly's eyes, did something to her she couldn't explain and didn't expect. Something that seemed like a very good antidote to all the anxiety wrapping itself round her lately.

As they said goodbye to the sheep and put all their rain gear back on to head back out into the downpour, Paul caught her eye for a moment and muttered, "Sprinkles. You fight dirty."

And then laughed. Audrey thought it the most infectious laugh she'd ever heard, and the three of them were soaked and giggling by the time they made it to her kitchen door.

Chapter Seven

For a man who sang the virtues of chocolate milk, even Paul thought Audrey's hot cocoa was overboard. And that was before the showering of sprinkles. He caught Audrey's wince when Lilly dumped—and *dumped* clearly was the verb in play here—a load of sprinkles onto the mound of whipped cream that already graced her mug. While he'd thought Audrey a bit much when she insisted Lilly put a plate under the mug—wouldn't a coaster be sufficient?—he didn't blame her now. The thing looked more like a dessert than a beverage. He had to admit, though, that the drink was really very good.

He was sipping the last of his now, feeling the sugar rush churn through him, watching Audrey teach Lilly to knit. Well, it didn't look like knitting, at least not as he remembered. Knitting, as far as he knew, involved two needles, and the thing in Lilly's hand looked like a spool with four nails on it.

"This is the best thing for someone your age," Audrey said as she had handed Lilly something she called a Knitting Nancy. True to the name, it looked more like a toy than a craft, and Paul supposed that was part of its charm. Basically, Lilly did something with yarn at the top, where the four nails were involved, and a "knitted" tube of yarn—sort of a giant, colorful shoelace—came out the bottom. It looked to Paul like a yarny version of sausage making, but he decided to keep that observation to himself, opting to watch the pair quietly.

They were entertaining. It was easy to see that Lilly's bois-terous, easily distracted personality—standard eight-year-old issue as far as Paul could tell—confounded Audrey. All the same, she stuck in there, her obsession for knitting winning out over her frustration at having to teach the same step eleven times over. It was at once so different from Caroline's natural maternal ease, and then again all too similar. He hadn't counted on Lilly's one-on-one interaction with another woman to unsettle him so.

Lilly ate it up. She sat there, her little pink tongue stuck out in absolute concentration, using the small hook Audrey had given her to make whatever loopy steps transformed the straight yarn to the tube of knitting that emerged out of the gadget. When she'd managed—with no small amount of do-overs and untangling from Audrey—to produce half a foot of tube, she held it up as if it were made of gold. "Look, Daddy! I knitted!"

Paul was broadsided by the lump in his throat. "Spiffy," he managed, hiding his emotion with a big gulp of hot choco-late, and getting a regrettable burn down his throat as a reward.

His eyes met Audrey's for a potent moment before she quickly busied herself with Lilly's latest tangle. She'd caught it, seen the crack in him. It made him feel exposed, vulnera-ble that he hadn't been able to sufficiently mask it. His grief was a highly private thing to him, something to be kept tucked away in a black box never to be publicly opened. Perhaps that was one of his motivations for moving—it was easier to keep the black box in hiding with people who hadn't seen him holding back the sobs at Caroline's funeral. Hadn't watched his heartbreaking inability to throw that first handful of dirt on Caroline's casket. He'd stood there for what felt like years, trying to launch her burial, utterly unable to do so. He'd felt as if his heart was ripped open for all the world to see when Caroline's mother had walked up, kissed Paul on his wet cheek and thrown a handful in his stead.

It helped that no one here knew that. Maybe it was necessary that no one here knew that. A survival basic of some sort.

"Now, what you've made here is called an i-cord. Make about two or three feet of this, and there's all kinds of things you can do with it. Next time, I'll even show you how to change colors and make stripes. And they make yarn that changes color all by itself, so the stripes are built in, too."

"I like stripes. Can we make polka-dots? They're my favorite."

Audrey laughed. "No, but you can wind up the i-cord into little spirals and put polka dots on things like sweaters or bags and such." She pointed to the contraption. "Show me you can do four rounds without my help, and you'll be all set."

Lilly bent over the task, Audrey over her shoulder, and Paul used the quiet to look around Audrey's kitchen. While it certainly contained much more than Paul's barely furnished house, no one could call it cluttered. The entire place was so tidy he suspected her spices were in alphabetical order. Perhaps even cataloged. He guessed the spoons in her silverware drawer were nestled in perfect rows. The kind of order, Paul thought, Lilly could undo in thirty seconds. An archway revealed a small section of her living room, which looked as tidy as everything else. The books on the bookshelf were lined up precisely—smallest to largest down the four shelves of volumes he could see. No wonder this woman was traumatized by the unexpected near tripling of her tidy flock of sheep. He wondered if there were any free-spirited librarians, for all the ones he'd ever met seemed to have Audrey's passion for order. Perhaps that was knitting's attraction for her—it seemed like an orderly, almost mathematical craft wrapped around all the artistic qualities of yarn.

Rather an esoteric thought for a guy chugging cocoa, he thought to himself. Maybe it was the writer finally emerging in him, this fascination with character and motive. Her long straight hair suited her no-nonsense attitude. Her lean face made the most of her enormous brown eyes and fair complexion. Audrey was a puzzle, a combination of expected and surprising characteristics he wanted to solve. He found himself paying attention to her interaction with Lilly in acute detail— the way she placed her hand on Lilly's to show her a technique, how she whispered in her ear, the funny way one dark eyebrow shot up when Lilly said something outrageous— which was entirely too often.

He was completely unaware of how much time had gone by until Audrey checked her watch and said, "Oh! It's nearly four! I need to feed the girls and get ready for choir practice." She popped up from the table and produced a neatly folded paper shopping bag from a cabinet. Paul mused she was the kind of person who folded and reused wrapping paper. "You take this home and let me know when you've got three feet made. Then we'll make something fun with it and you can try stripes next. Got it?" She extracted—and that was the word for it, for Lilly was clutching the knitting thing to her chest—the yarn and supplies from Lilly and arranged them in the bag. "Don't let them get wet on your way home, and don't let the yarn get tangled."

"Thanks for letting her borrow the…whatever you call it," Paul said, taking his own mug to the counter and fetching Lilly's sloshy mug and plate, as well.

"Knitting Nancy. And Lilly can keep it." Audrey shrugged. "I own six."

"Five now." Paul smiled. "That's very kind of you." He looked at Lilly. "What do you say?"

"Can I come back tomorrow?" Lilly piped up, clutching her bag.

"Start with 'thank you,' missy." Paul used his "daddy voice."

"Thank-you-and-can-I-come-back-tomorrow?" Lilly mashed the sentence together into a single urgent word. Paul felt he was giving Audrey the hundredth "sorry about that" look of their short acquaintance.

Audrey leaned down. "You may come back after you've made three feet. That's our deal. You keep your part of the bargain, and I'll keep mine."

Paul realized that if he was very fortunate, Audrey Lupine might just have given him maybe sixty minutes of a quietly occupied Lilly. That was worth running out in the rain to coddle sheep any day. He nodded at his new ally. "You make a mean hot chocolate."

"I never make a claim without the evidence to back it up." Her words were serious, but her smile was close to joking.

"Mizz Madison says you have the prettiest voice in Middleburg. Is that why you go to choir?"

"I like to sing," Audrey said, a blush tinting her pale complexion. "But as for that claim, well, you can just tell Ms. Madison I thank her for the compliment."

She sang. Very well, evidently.

Paul couldn't quite put his finger on why that stuck with him so. He found himself spending half the night—through dinner and homework and as Knitting Nancy was put through more of her paces—wondering what Audrey Lupine's singing voice sounded like.

In between patrons, Audrey spent Friday afternoon staring at the pile of applications in front of her. Applications. To march in a parade. Even with her love of organization, she'd thought the application process unnecessary at first. Sandy Burnside, a woman Howard had once called "a blond tornado" but who was actually the driving energy behind lots of what made Middleburg the charming town it was, wanted no process at all. "Why can't we keep it at build a float, line up your folks and show up on Saturday morning?" she asked. That was the moment Howard chose to put Audrey in charge of the Easter Parade. Come to think of it, Audrey had absolutely no memory of Howard even asking her if she wanted to do it—he just declared her chairmanship on the spot. Back then, a part of her was flattered by the appointment. That part was quickly squelched by the tidal wave of detail Howard demanded, and his considerable lack of delegation skills. As in the man delegated nothing. *Micromanaging* was putting it kindly. Truth be told, Howard's greatest mayoral talent was to dream up enormous projects and then tell other people exactly how to accomplish them.

Her first victory was editing Howard's four—yes, four-page—application draft to two sides of one sheet. In this case, however, Howard's love of detail had actually done her a favor—she basically had the entire parade in front of her on paper. Howard had convinced her to look through the applications before she said no to organizing the parade.

Howard was no fool, for as she studied the applications and sorted them into types of entries—musical groups, civic clubs, display floats and something which could only be classified as "other," it seemed almost doable. The "other" section couldn't help but pique her interest. Exactly what would Vern Murphy's "precision riding mower brigade" do? And if Howard rode in the Middleburg Community Church float— as the application stated he would—then who would be Grand

Marshal? Or—and Audrey shuddered at the irrational but highly likely thought—would Howard try to do both?

After a half hour of sorting, re-sorting and just plain brainstorming, Audrey came up with what she hoped was a brilliant plan. She moved her lunch hour to 3:00 p.m., made two phone calls and walked over to the town hall in the afternoon to set it in motion.

"I'll do it," Audrey pronounced as she settled herself into Howard's mayoral office with Sandy Burnside beside her.

"I knew you would," Howard said, leaning back in his chair.

"Well, I didn't," Sandy countered, looking relieved. "Honestly, I thought y'all called me in here to hand the whole thing over to me."

"You didn't let me finish," Audrey said. "I was going to say I'll do it on three conditions."

"Am I gonna like what I'm about to hear?" Sandy narrowed her eyes.

Audrey wasn't sure. The only thing she did know was that Sandy was just about the only force that could keep Howard in check and, conversely, Howard was just about the only thing that stopped Sandy's enthusiasm from running rampant all over Middleburg. Audrey had often mused that, while the town would never admit it, Middleburg had two judicial branches: Howard and Sandy. Audrey was just going to use this system of checks and balances to her advantage.

"Howard, I'll run the Easter Parade, but only if Sandy is in charge of choosing the Grand Marshal." This maneuver deftly assured that neither Sandy nor Howard could be the Grand Marshal, for neither one would let the other do something that would appear so self-serving. Sandy would lap up the whole selection process precisely because it would be filled with all the interpersonal stuff she loved, and Howard would be spending his energies trying to influence Sandy's decision rather than ordering Audrey around. Plus, it simply had to be said: Sandy and Howard were such obvious choices that Audrey thought she'd find the whole process of figuring out who else should be Marshal vastly entertaining—provided she wasn't in charge of it, which, in a few minutes, she wouldn't be. It was brilliant.

"Me? In charge of choosing the Grand Marshal?" Sandy looked surprised, but pleased. "I'd think you'd want to do that yourself."

"Seems to me this is really more your kind of thing," Audrey said. "My strengths are in the details, not the big picture."

After a moment's thought, Sandy planted hands—graced, as always, with long pink fingernails—on Howard's desk. "I'd be delighted."

Now Howard was cornered. If he said no, it would be clear he was only objecting to Sandy—something he'd never admit. But by approving Sandy, he knew he'd not be Grand Marshal—something she'd never allow. Exactly as Audrey had planned it. Middleburg's longtime mayor folded his hands across his midsection. "I don't really see how I can say no."

Audrey found his choice of words interesting, if not downright satisfying, so she moved forward. "My second condition is that the fifteen-dollar application fee go toward the library's literacy program. We need the money, and since no one's given a thought where that money should go, I've decided."

"Honestly, I don't know why we even charged anybody to walk in a parade anyhow," Sandy said, eyeing Howard. "Seems silly. We don't charge to walk down our street any other day."

"We wanted only serious applicants," Howard explained.

"Serious applicants," Sandy echoed incredulously. "To walk in a parade. Really, Howard, you outdo yourself."

Those two would be at each other in a matter of seconds if she didn't do something. "So you agree to my proposal?"

"Well, I don't know," Howard replied slowly. "I haven't heard condition number three yet."

"You both sit on the library board. So I'm asking you, now, to make a motion approving my hours to go down to part-time during the three weeks my ewes are lambing. That's the only way I'll agree to everything else." Audrey sat back in her chair, hands clasped, and waited.

"I think that's reasonable," Sandy said, daring Howard to think otherwise.

"Well..." Howard stalled.

"Oh, Howard, lighten up. It's not like lives are at stake here." At Audrey's slightly shocked expression, she added, "Well, human lives. I think it's the least we can do, given all you've asked of her." She emphasized the *you*.

It took twenty minutes more of posturing, but in the end, it was Demanding World, 0 ; Audrey, 1.

Chapter Eight

Audrey walked back to the library with a smile on her face and a prayer of thanksgiving in her heart. Perhaps God really was going to take her hand and lead her through this crazy season. After all, if she could manage Howard Epson and Sandy Burnside, a flock of sheep might just be within her reach. And that massive budget report due today by five should be a cakewalk for a woman of her newfound organizational confidence.

She opened the library door to find Lilly Sycamore sitting in front of her desk, her little blue coat zipped right up to her chin and tears in her enormous blue eyes. Lilly held a tangled wad of yarn with the Knitting Nancy's painted head poking out.

"Daddy and Nancy had a fight," Lilly said in a wobbly voice.

Paul's eyes broadcast "Save me!" from over Lilly's shoulder. "We're sort of stuck. I know you've got work to do but…"

Lilly's eyes filled with enormous, heart-wrenching tears. That wobbling lower lip had more persuasive powers that Sandy and Howard combined. Audrey checked her watch. "I've still got ten minutes left on my lunch hour. Let's see if we can't get Nancy up and running. I can write down the instructions for your dad in case you get stuck again, okay?"

The disaster looked worse than it actually was. The solution was simple, but Paul must have assumed it was complicated because he'd done all kinds of things in his attempts to fix it. She showed both of them what had gone wrong, how to spot it again and how to fix it. Lilly actually had a knack for it, grasping the concepts right away. She guessed they'd graduate to real knitting by next week, if not sooner. Paul looked mostly embarrassed at having to ask for help of any kind, much less a knitting rescue.

She knew his attention was driven by the need to help his daughter, but Audrey couldn't help feeling watched. As if his concentration was more fascination than obligation—which was a notion that got under her skin entirely too quickly. She found herself talking too much, a nervous habit she hated, which only served to make her more nervous and chatter even more. While she was mortified by her own behavior, Paul and Lilly seemed to find it amusing. She was sure Paul laughed at her poor jokes just to be polite, sure Lilly asked questions just to be silly. It didn't take long at all to get Knitting Nancy back to full production speed, Lilly's little fingers flying over the task with an attention Audrey had to respect. When Lilly produced a tape measure from her little knitting bag and showed she had only two inches left on her three-foot goal, Audrey could only smile.

"I owe you one," Paul said when Lilly finally wiggled down from the chair to skip off to the children's room for a few minutes. "Actually," he said, stuffing his hands in his pockets, "I owe you three. Do you know I wrote a whole chapter last night while Lilly got seven inches of knitting done? I haven't had that much peace and quiet in our house in ages. If I ever get published, I might have to list you in the acknowledgments."

"And how is the spy novel coming along?" She had actually browsed through the books-in-print listings the other day, looking to see if any horse-oriented spy novels had been published in recent years. She wasn't sure why; it was mostly a lark to see if someone had beaten Paul to the punch on his unusual setting idea.

He gave a lopsided grin. "Slow. I have to say, I thought it'd be easier than this. When I was working, it was like I couldn't stop the ideas from coming at me all day long. Now, I sit and stare at that white page and wonder who made off with my imagination."

He had a disarming smile, unassuming and genuine. She suspected his slow, steady nature made him a very good vet— the kind of person who'd be the coolest head in the room when a crisis hit. She was charmed that he'd devoted such energy to untangling Lilly's knitting. She didn't know too many men who would have put up with that. Then again, she didn't know too many eight-year-olds with Lilly's persistence. "I imagine you'll grow into a rhythm of some sort," she offered to Paul. "I used to think I'd love to knit all day if I didn't have to work, then one day I broke my leg and had to sit all day long. It's the one and only time I got sick of knitting. Everything in moderation, I suppose."

"Except whipped cream and sprinkles. Those, Lilly has informed me, should always be used in heaps."

Audrey laughed. "I guess I taught her more than knitting, hmm?" How many times had she chuckled at the memory of Lilly's wide eyes when she'd placed the overtopped cocoa in front of her? She had gone overboard, too, with a silliness that felt as refreshing as it felt foreign. Truth be told, children often exasperated Audrey, all wild messiness and untamed energy, but somehow Lilly had captured a corner of her heart. She couldn't even say why. It would only be fair to say

Audrey *tolerated* children, despite their being a staple of library patronage. She'd been smart enough to recruit a small corps of volunteers to staff the children's section of the library, keeping her need to cope with them down to a minimum. She'd been asked to teach Sunday school or direct the church's children's choir, but always found a reason to decline. It had no appeal whatsoever.

Gram had never fretted about her "undomestic character" as Mama had called it during one particularly nasty argument, but in truth, Audrey felt like it made her different than every other woman in Middleburg. They all pined after husbands and babies, it seemed. Audrey never wanted to settle for anything less than a sweeping, epic, Jane-Austen-worthy kind of love—and the prospects of *that* showing up in tiny little Middleburg required more optimism than Audrey possessed. The truth was, she'd grown comfortable in the ordered life she'd made. The more baffling truth was that somewhere, deep down, she didn't resent Lilly—and the sheep and even Paul— for knocking it all to pieces.

Paul looked her straight in the eye. "I'll help with your sheep however I can." She knew, by the way he said it, that he meant it. And she knew that it was not a comfortable thing for him to offer, either. He was making an exception for her, going back on a promise to himself. That got under her skin, too, and she didn't know what to do with it.

"Thanks," she said simply, afraid to take the conversation further.

She didn't have to, because at that moment Lilly came back with a stack of books. Each one about sheep. She hadn't realized the Middleburg Community Library owned that many sheep-themed books, but by the size of the stack, Lilly had unearthed every single one. Audrey guessed the volunteer in the children's room this afternoon was collapsed on a chair panting about now.

"That's a whole lot of books. And you haven't returned last week's yet."

"I'm not done with them, but I want these." Lilly dumped the stack on Audrey's desk with a wide grin.

"I think that's great, but we do have limits. We need enough books for everybody." Audrey leaned down until she was face-to-face with Lilly. "You pick three of these, and promise me you'll bring back the other ones from last week tomorrow, and we'll call it even."

"Aww," Lilly moaned.

"Miss Audrey's been really nice to you today, fixing your knitting and all," Paul reminded his daughter. "You'll be at three feet soon, and you'll want her to show you all those things she promised the other night, right? I think we ought to do exactly what she says."

"Only three?" Lilly pouted. "I like 'em all."

"I'm glad, but three's my final offer."

The Serious Father Authority Voice came out. "Three, Lillian."

Lilly selected three and handed them over with the sort of look Audrey imagined small children normally reserved for brussels sprouts. "Smart decision." Audrey surprised herself by giving Lilly a conspiratorial wink. "Besides, the rest'll be here when you're ready for them. Who knew we had such a big sheep collection?"

Audrey couldn't remember having more victories in a single afternoon. Maybe the torrent of tasks before her wouldn't be so bad after all.

"Ruth's coughing again. And you know what they say…when sheep get sick, they go really quickly. What if Dusty had some sort of virus and she caught it?"

Paul had already regretted his "I'll help in any way"

remark, and it hadn't even been twenty-four hours. "What did your vet say?"

"He told me to stop worrying." Paul suspected, based on the level of exasperation in Audrey's voice, that he'd been a bit stronger than that.

"I concur. You said they've had all their shots. She probably just ate something that didn't agree with her."

"She's pregnant. She can't get sick now. I looked it up, and I found four diseases she can get that could cause her to lose the lambs. Her gums look funny to me. They should be paler, shouldn't they?"

There were days when Paul just hated the Internet. An educated client was a good thing. A hyperinformed panicked neighbor to whom he owed a favor was quite another. At least it wasn't raining this time. Chapter four had been flowing so well this morning he almost didn't answer his phone when it rang, but Lilly was at school and he hadn't gotten caller ID installed on his phone. Yet. "I'll be over in ten minutes," he'd said.

Paul wasn't surprised to find the sheep in good health. Pregnant and irritable, maybe, but nothing requiring a vet's visit. It was time to offer Audrey a little perspective. "How many times have you called Dr. Vickers this week?" When she acquired a guilty look, he pressed the point as gently as he could. "Really."

For a moment she looked just like Lilly did when caught misbehaving. "Four."

Paul sighed. "Your vet's a good sport for putting up with that, but I'm guessing even he has his limits, Audrey. You want to be on his good side now, so when you need him for lambing you haven't used up all his patience. I'm telling you, as a friend, you're going to have to find a way to be less panicked about your sheep."

"I know that," she said, pacing the barn. "I know. I look at you, and you're so calm, so in control about Lilly, and I don't know how you do it. I can't seem to stop worrying about them. I feel so responsible for them."

"Look, I admire that, and you've taken good care of them so far, but there is such a thing as too much care. God knew what He was doing when He made sheep, and they come with all the necessary equipment." She didn't even laugh at his joke, small as it was. He caught her by the arm as she began to pace again. "They're going to be *fine,* Audrey. But not if you make yourself sick worrying over them." He hadn't even realized he'd touched her until she froze in her tracks. They stood there, both startled by the contact, and Paul was sure even the sheep looked up and took notice. "You've got to calm down," he said gruffly, pulling his hand away and stuffing it in his pants pocket. "For everyone's sake," he added when the barn still seemed far too silent.

"I don't know how," she said quietly after a long moment had passed.

The need in her voice undid something in his chest. He leaned up against the barn wall and ran his hands down his face. It would be okay to tell her. It might help. "When Caroline—my wife—was in chemo, I couldn't seem to stop worrying. If it would work. How she'd hold up. What the whole thing would do to Lilly. A little girl should just never have to see her mother that sick, you know? It got to the point where I'd worry all the time. Where all I saw or felt or knew was the worry."

"I'm so sorry." Audrey sat down on a crate, her eyes fixed on him with such a tender sadness. It was always so awful to tell people about it the first time.

"But then Caroline started worrying about me instead of focusing all her attention on getting well. So, you see, I was only making things worse. My worry gave her more to worry about. It was wrong to do that to her. And I realized, when my pastor and I talked about it, that it was wrong to do that to God. We had so many people praying over Caroline and our family. Worrying was like saying to God and all those praying people that I didn't trust them." He looked at Audrey. "I'll pray for you and your sheep. I'll get my Bible study to pray for you and your sheep. You get the choir and your friends to do likewise. And you do the best you can to believe you're supposed to have eleven sheep and God hasn't just looked the other way while you've messed up. Deal?"

"Deal."

Chapter Nine

Audrey sat Lilly right next to her on the couch, holding the two needles in front of her. "It looks hard, and you'll feel like your fingers are getting all tangled up, but that's only at first. Watch me." She went about making a knit stitch, going very slowly. The thick, bright yarn and big needles had been the perfect choice to lure Lilly's attention—she couldn't help herself when she saw them at her favorite yarn shop in Lexington last week. And, they had little sheep figures on the ends—what could be more perfect?

"I think I get it." Lilly took the yarn and needles into her own hands. Slowly, with considerable effort, she worked her smaller fingers as Audrey talked her through the steps of the stitch. When she finished the stitch and slipped it from one needle to the other, Lilly beamed. "Did I get it right?"

Audrey's memory cast back to the warm summer afternoons on Gram's porch, fumbling her way through her first knitting projects. Was her current smile as warm and proud as Gram's had been? Had she been as excited to make her first row as Lilly looked? "Perfect," she encouraged the charming girl. "Now try the next one."

She watched as Lilly pursed her lips in concentration, repeating out loud the instructions Audrey had said on the stitch before. Audrey looked up for a split second, to see if Paul noticed his daughter's accomplishment. He was staring at the two of them, a bittersweet and complicated expression filling his features.

"Is that right?" Lilly's needles jutted back into Audrey's vision.

"Yes, but try pulling just a bit after each stitch. Not too much, just a bit. Use your index finger, like this." Audrey took back the needles and demonstrated on a handful of stitches. "It'll help make them even."

"Okay." Lilly bent her head over the project again, and Audrey felt Paul watching them. It was an odd sensation, an awareness, startling but not unpleasant. She felt her gaze pulled up, not really wanting to look at him but unable to resist the urge.

He had the most expressive eyes. She could read a dozen thoughts in the way he looked at her before he looked back down to his newspaper. Fascination mixed with caution. Warmth held at a distance. She wasn't quite sure how the blue of his eyes could be so pure and complex at the same time. Even glancing down, she felt as if she could still see his eyes. The tingle at the back of her neck told her he wasn't really reading the paper. Any more than she was inspecting Lilly's stitches—something she really ought to be doing.

Lilly, however, due to either hours at the Knitting Nancy or simply a natural knack for it, finished her row with perfect, if uneven stitches. "Wow," Audrey admired, "I've taught grown-ups whose first rows looked worse." She forced herself to count to ten before giving in to the urge to look up again.

And met his eyes, again. They held her gaze for a moment, catching Audrey's breath, and despite several momentary flickers away—mostly driven by what her pulse was doing to her train of thought—her eyes continued to stray back to his. It was a moment too fragile for a smile, too unsettling to last long, but too important to ignore. Out of the corner of her eyes, she noticed Paul's grip on the newspaper tighten. It made Audrey wish she'd brought knitting of her own, something to do with her hands and somewhere else to put her eyes.

"Dad, look!" Lilly held up her second row, thankfully breaking off the moment.

"Looks good to me. Seems you're a natural."

"She is," Audrey agreed, entirely too quickly, feeling as though her voice pitched up half an octave. "This looks great. Now turn your work like this—" she demonstrated how to flip the working needle to the other hand "—and start over, just like before."

"I'm knitting, Dad. It's not as hard as I thought."

"Looks hard," Paul said, one tawny eyebrow dubiously raised.

"All knitting is two basic stitches done over and over. With a few fancy tricks thrown in now and then. You'll see. Okay, now, you do this row all by yourself without any help from me." It was the way Audrey always taught, but she instantly realized it left her one entire row of Lilly's with nothing to do. Suddenly it seemed as if two hundred stitches were on that needle instead of just twenty.

Paul seemed to sense her unease. "You want a cup of tea or something? Lilly had me buy some at the store last week." A flush tinted his face momentarily, realizing the sort of admission that was. Paul didn't drink tea, which meant they'd bought it to host her. Well, she had promised to teach Lilly to knit, so she really shouldn't read too much into that. It was the hospitable thing to do.

So why did the gesture touch her so? Millions of people buy tea every day, but she couldn't discount the tiny spark in his eye when he talked about buying tea for her. "Lilly asked me to," he repeated again, as if needing to retreat to safer ground.

"Tea would be nice," she replied, feeling her own face heat up. She'd probably have choked down strong black coffee if he'd offered it with that look in his eyes.

"Me, too," Lilly chimed in as her father folded the paper and got up from his chair.

Paul offered a lopsided smile and shrugged. "Lilly drinks tea now."

Audrey offered an apologetic wince, sure Lilly's new beverage preference had been her doing. "Not cocoa?" she inquired, almost afraid to hear the answer.

Paul's reply was a self-deprecating smirk. "I've been usurped."

Audrey wanted to cringe. She couldn't tell from his expression and his tone if he was upset or found the whole thing funny.

"What's that mean?" Lilly asked.

"It means I own a teapot now and I'm man enough to use it." He supplied a cavemanish grunt and lumbered over to touch a finger to Lilly's nose. It was the first time Audrey had seen Paul joke with Lilly, and it charmed her, even if it did feel too close. He touched his daughter so tenderly, just inches away, with such a twinkle in his eye. "So y'all better watch out," he added, mocking a Kentucky twang to rather poor effect.

"Dad," Lilly giggled. "We don't say 'y'all.'"

"Not *yet,*" he called as he entered the kitchen.

Lilly had finally put down her knitting and agreed to go to bed. Fixated as she could get on things, Paul knew he had a potential fight on his hands for things like chores and homework now that her fascination had fixed on knitting. Still, it was hard to knock a quiet, portable and creative pastime that gave Paul some time to get serious work done when Lilly was at home and awake. Up until now, school and the handful of hours after her bedtime were enough to keep him on schedule, but all of that could go out the window when summer came.

Writing full-time was proving harder than he thought. Back in practice, Paul would thirst for the hour or two he could put into a writing project, eager to get his ideas down on paper. Now, he had more time than ideas. It was excruciating to stare at a blank page. Not that he had any deadlines other than the ones he'd set for himself—first draft done by June—but he was used to being productive. Getting things done. Ticking off a long list of tasks each day. Now, he was the creative equivalent of "all dressed up and nowhere to go."

Yeah, right, Paul thought to himself as the white of tonight's blank page blared out at him. *You keep telling yourself that.* It was far easier to think of himself as having writer's block than the unsettling truth that he was distracted.

By Audrey Lupine.

I'm not ready for this. He found his fingers typing the blurt of a thought, the blank page suddenly becoming a letter to God. He did that, wrote many of his prayers as long letters to his Lord. It helped him focus his thoughts and look back on insights. He stared at the sentence, changing the period at the end to a comma and adding, am I?

I can't go back, he wrote, sighing.

I'm a vet to her, and I want to leave that behind. I need
a new me, a chance to start over. Lord, I'm worried that
if I keep going over to her barn, I'll just slip back into
the old me and all this will be lost.

All that was true, but it wasn't what was keeping him from his novel. What kind of idiocy was it to try and skirt the issue in a letter to God? He tried to turn off his inner editor, the one who told him not to write certain things, and just let it come purely out his fingertips. A purging. Taking a deep breath, he mentally dived in and typed. Watching her tonight, something bubbled up. Describe it, he told himself, as a writer's exercise. Get it out, down on the page, then you can move on to that scene you need to get done.

Her fingers have a practical grace. More honest than elegant, but there's something about the way her hands move. Over the yarn, pushing her hair out of her eyes when she looks down, around a teacup. She looks so in control, but there's this caution I see underneath—it shows up in her fingers to me, somehow. Her eyes have authority, a stubborn determination that I think the rest of the world sees easily. I see it, too—especially with the sheep. Her eyes are so dark, like you'd never see the bottom of them no matter how hard you looked. People would probably call them lovely or dramatic, but it's her hands I keep staring at. Watching them hold Lilly's hands caught me by surprise. I couldn't look away. I was clear across the room and yet I felt their movement, felt them rest on my daughter, my flesh and blood, Caroline's pale skin and long fingers. It felt like worlds colliding, watching Audrey touch Lilly. Not because it hurt, but because it didn't.

He'd somehow moved back into this letter to God, the need to sort out his reaction overshadowing any attempt at description.

It didn't hurt, Lord. I wasn't ready for that. I felt...

He paused, physically afraid to type the word.

…drawn. To her. The very beginnings of something I
haven't felt in a long time. There's too much on my plate
now, Lord, to add this. Lilly isn't settled, I don't want
to be distracted from this new work You're calling me
to, but that's just what I am—distracted.

He pulled his hands from the keyboard to glance around
the room, as if he'd just made some earth-shattering confes-
sion and the world surely heard it. Only the silence of the
den surrounded him. He debated whether to go on, wanting
to go deeper and wanting to run from it at the same time. He
looked up, seeing a lit upper-story window on her house
from where he sat at his desk.

She was awake. Well, of course she was awake; it was
only ten o'clock and not past anybody's bedtime at her
house. Unbidden, an image of Audrey, bent over a diary
penning an entry in long, flowing script—a detail for which
he had absolutely no evidence—invaded his brain. He
wondered, against every impulse not to, if she would write
an entry about teaching Lilly to knit. She looked as if she
enjoyed it so much, as if her enthusiasm was seeping out to
him from across the room. Lilly's utter absorption—wanting
to stay up late to "get another row done"—hadn't helped his
own preoccupation. He just kept seeing her hands writing
"Lilly" this and "Lilly" that.

I need to stay away, he wrote, then underlined it.

I'm not sure of that sort of thing right now, I'm
probably vulnerable because of the anniversary. I'm
confusing her niceness to Lilly with something else.

Guard me, Lord, because I don't feel very wise at the moment. Just guard me.

He was going to write *be my Shepherd,* but it seemed counterproductive.

Chapter Ten

Paul took another look at Lilly's math homework over breakfast. Her grades had gone down again. Fractions were rough on anyone, but Lilly's preoccupation with Audrey's sheep and knitting had made schoolwork a daily argument between Paul and his daughter. She'd fallen into a regular after-school routine of helping Audrey with the ewes, raking straw and setting out water and such for the animals who were beginning to need more and more care. He was proud of her, but it was easy to see where all this was heading. Once the lambs came, things would only get worse. Tasks would multiply. And what young girl could resist all that fluffy cuteness when it posed such a potent distraction to math facts?

"Lilly," he began, trying not to start yet another round of the same argument, "half of these are wrong."

"I don't care!" Lilly pouted, pushing angrily at her eggs. "I hate math!"

"You can hate it all you want, but it won't get your homework done."

"No one *needs* math."

He was in no mood to get into this again, especially before

school. "Lots of people need math. Even Miss Audrey said she uses it in her knitting, remember?" Spurred by the reference, he stole a glance over to Lilly's knitting basket. She'd done another six inches on her scarf last night. Instead of her assigned reading, he suspected. Paul was beginning to want to look this particular gift sheep in the mouth—Lilly was far too prone to neglecting her schoolwork in favor of getting a few more rows done. "Did you do your reading yet?"

She didn't answer. Paul looked at his watch. Not enough time to get anything done now.

"No heading over to Miss Audrey's this afternoon until your homework is done. *Including* your reading."

Lilly produced the exasperated eye-roll of which she was a master. "Aww, Daaad!"

Caroline was always so much better at this. "School has to come before sheep. I don't want to regret letting you help her, but you're going to have to do your part." To punctuate his declaration, Paul took the basket of her knitting and put it up into one of the kitchen cabinets. It made him feel like a big bad monster taking away her toys, but only fools negotiated with second graders.

She slammed down her fork and stomped off to her room. Getting her on the bus this morning would be a battle. Again. *Grant me wisdom, Lord. And patience. And endurance. And the memory of how to do common denominators.*

As Audrey got ready for work a few weeks later, she surveyed the box of bottles, nipples, heat lamps and medicines that sat in her mudroom waiting to be put into service. Lambing was coming. In two weeks, she'd start her stint of reduced hours that would last until the week after Easter—useful for both the parade and lambing duties ahead of her. The ewes' bellies were rounding out, and Audrey was sure she saw the happy glow of motherhood in their faces. Everything was falling into place. She found herself humming the swelling classic hymn "The Lamb of God" as she walked out to the barn door for a check on the girls before leaving for the library.

The sound stopped her first. A dreadful, moaning bleat, not at all like the normal sounds she knew from her ewes. It was like Martha's bleat, and then not at all like her voice. Was she sick? In labor somehow and already in trouble? The overwhelming sense of "wrongness" hit her like a solid wall, sending Audrey into a flat-out run toward the pen. The girls were huddled in one corner, facing away from her.

Three of them.

"Oh, Lord, no…" Audrey moaned aloud, her fears confirmed. She pushed her way gently through the trio to find Martha lying on the bedding. Her first thought was that Martha was sick or had died, but Martha swung her head around at Audrey's approach. Audrey would have argued to anyone, looking in Martha's eyes, that sheep could cry. The tiny pink mass Martha was licking and nuzzling was, without a doubt, the saddest thing Audrey had ever seen. A stillborn lamb was just *wrong,* a violation of hope that stabbed into Audrey's chest like a knife. She grabbed the side of the pen for support, trying to push out the sob and pull in the gasp that tangled in her throat. Martha hadn't dug the ground or swelled or shown any of the signs of labor. This was weeks before she should have given birth. It couldn't be happening. Not to Martha. Martha was the only ewe not having twins, according to Dr. Vickers. The one *supposed* to be pregnant. It seemed so horribly unfair.

The other ewes knew. They surrounded her, breathing softly in a scene that seemed the terrible negative image of the Bethlehem stable—the animals gathered around death instead of life. Not Martha. Martha nudged the contorted, stained body and Audrey felt her legs give way. There had to be something she could do. Audrey dragged her mind through all the research, knowing she'd read about what to do but completely unable to recall it. A wave of helpless sobs overtook her, and she touched Martha's soft, pink ear, moaning "I'm sorry" over and over.

When she caught her breath, she reached into her pocket and called Paul on her cell phone. The shred of composure she gained evaporated when she heard his voice. "Come." She could barely get the word out. "Come now!"

"Audrey? What's wrong? Is it the girls?" She could hear his steps, hear him rushing out the door with the cell phone in his hand.

"It's Martha. Oh, Paul, come now."

Paul burst through the door not half a minute later, his breath puffing mist into the chilled morning air.

It took him ten seconds to guess the situation, and she watched his heart break inside his eyes. "Oh, no. Not Martha."

The vet in him took over, scanning the pen for details, running his hands over Martha's body and assessing her health, inspecting the stillborn lamb with tender reverence. He straightened up slowly, reaching back for Audrey's hand even before he turned to her. When he pulled Audrey into his arms, the last of her control fled and she cried in great, heaving sobs onto his shoulder.

"I'm sorry," he said, stroking her hair with the same grief she had stroked Martha's ear. "I'm sorry."

"I failed her." Audrey made herself say it, even though the words stabbed like broken glass. "I was so busy watching the ewes with twins I must not have seen her in trouble. I missed the signs. Not even when I checked before I went to bed last night. I didn't *see.*"

"Sometimes lambs just don't make it. There aren't always signs."

Audrey could only shake her head; words couldn't find their way above the weight pressing down upon her. She'd failed Martha. Martha, who was supposed to be the mother. How awfully, preventably wrong it all seemed. Martha's eyes looked empty beyond imagination. She'd even stopped tending to the little sheep and now stared off into nowhere, silent and spent.

Somehow, Paul maneuvered Audrey onto a bench and then opened up the storage chest in the corner to pull out a towel. With a carefulness that was almost too hard to watch, he picked up the tiny body and wrapped it in the towel, wiping the muck from the delicate face. He had the quiet composure of a man too well acquainted with death. It made sense, suddenly, why the lambs had proved an irresistible draw for him and Lilly. Death needed to know life still survived.

He brought the bundle to Audrey. "There's no signs of disease, but I need to make sure Martha's okay. I'll take this for you, if you want."

She couldn't let him spare her the darker tasks of this. Not after all he'd been through. "No," she said, finding her voice surprisingly steady even as tears rolled down her cheeks. "I'll hold it."

"Him," he said, his voice breaking a bit. "It was a male."

The baby lamb was so heavy, as if death poured weight into the lifeless body. It felt important to hold it. To not back away from the tragic details just because they were unpleasant and painful. "Death happens on the farm," Dr. Vickers had always warned her. Somehow, she'd always thought her little flock too small to see death. Her sheep were supposed to be all about comfort and hope. Martha's little lamb stole her sense of control, knocking her off the precarious balance she'd managed to find in the past few weeks.

She wasn't sure how long it was before Paul returned—

time knotted around her as she cradled the bundle on her lap, listening to the way the three other sheep bleated softly as Paul moved through the barn. He walked into Audrey's house without asking, returning with the lambing kit he'd helped her pack and store in the mudroom. He treated Martha with things from the kit and with things from his vet bag, and Audrey felt as though she ought to take notes but couldn't move to find pen and paper. Paul knew what he was doing. He quickly checked over the other sheep, put out their morning feed, and then very gently took the bundle from Audrey's lap. "I'll handle this later. Martha is in good shape—the other girls are, too. We need to get you inside."

She couldn't make her legs move. Part of her knew she was taking all this too hard, that any farmer knew things like this happened all the time and she should be able to handle this, but her body felt as empty as Martha's hollow black eyes.

"Audrey…" Paul's voice was as gentle as his touch. "Come inside. We've done everything there is to do out here. Time will do the rest."

Chapter Eleven

Paul guided Audrey into her kitchen, where she slumped into a chair and stared quietly at the place mat. He knew that stunned, hollow feeling. He also knew there was nothing for it. Nothing but time, that is. Thank goodness Lilly was already at school. He let Audrey be while he found the kettle and put on water for tea. She didn't move while he opened a few cabinets in search of tea bags and sugar. He badly needed another strong cup of coffee, but there was no way he was going to leave her alone for the sake of a better shot of caffeine. Settling for what looked like the strongest brew—and that was an overstatement at best—he sat down beside her while the water heated up.

"I know it's just a lamb…" she said quietly, as if lecturing herself out of the grief. Trouble was, grief never really cared much about logic.

"It's not just a lamb." He kept his tone as soft as hers. "It was a life. It was important to you."

She looked up at him, surprise in her eyes. "They are. They're so important to me. That's sort of sad when you think about it. My best friends are *sheep*."

Her sincerity brought a small chuckle out of him. "I happen to know you have lots of friends. Several without four legs. And they'd all understand how hard this is for you."

She looked at him, eyes narrowing in that analytical squint he recognized from when she went over Cameron's endless spreadsheets or her own piles of research. "How did you do it?"

"Do what?"

"Survive Caroline's death. Get yourself and Lilly through something so awful." She plucked a tissue from a ceramic container lined up on the sideboard behind her. At that moment, she looked frail and small and very young—nothing at all like the stern librarian who lectured Lilly about standing on her books that first day. "This is just a lamb and I want to curl up in a ball and never talk to anyone again. How did you survive losing Caroline?"

"I felt like that for days afterward. I was so grateful Caroline had made her own decisions about her funeral and all that because I wanted the world to disappear that first week. I don't think I was a very good father. Caroline's and my parents stepped in and took care of most of the funeral details and Lilly while I was in that first fog. After that, you just sort of slog through the pain." It surprised him how easily he could talk about it with her. "I'd pray for God to get me through the next hour. The next ten minutes. And then ten minutes became ten days, ten days became ten weeks. When someone said I'd make friends with the pain, I thought they were nuts. But that's sort of how it is. It becomes a part of you, every day. You find a few happy things that sort of cancel it out for a while. And then a few more, and a few more." He leaned back in the chair. "And one day you turn around and two years have passed, and you realize you've somehow managed to scrape your life back together."

"You should be so proud. You've done a marvelous job

with Lilly. And you're writing—I think that's really wonderful." She sniffled and gave out a wobbly sigh. "I'm not much for kids, you know, but I really like Lilly."

They did have some special connection, those two. "She talks about you all the time. You've made quite an impression." It struck him, watching the tears glisten in her huge brown eyes, that he was talking about himself as much as Lilly. He'd kept telling himself Audrey was always in his thoughts at Lilly's prompting, but that wasn't true. He'd actually been frightened of how much he thought about Audrey. As if that were some sort of insult to Caroline's memory. But here, talking about Caroline to Audrey, he felt the counterbalance he'd just described—new joys coming to live alongside the grief. The impulse to take her hand both surprised and frightened him. He'd held her in the barn on pure human instinct— disaster's instant compassion—but this impulse was so unexpected and foreign he'd forgotten it could still exist inside him. He stared at her for a moment, baffled and cautious but unable to look away. She returned his gaze, and he thought he saw his own heart's discord reflected in her eyes.

The teakettle saved them, and he bolted off the chair for the safety of the kitchen counter. The previous moment's delicacy became lost under a mound of awkward hospitality. Suddenly they were avoiding each other's eyes and staying calculated distances apart, and he didn't know what to do with that. "You should call Dr. Vickers soon, let him know what's happened." He said it with entirely too clinical a tone.

"He had a cold earlier this week. I don't know if he can come out. Does he need to, now?" The word *now* held so much weight when she said it.

"That's up to him. But he needs to know, all the same. I could call the library for you, let them know. That is, if you want me to." Paul wanted to whack his forehead for making such a lame offer. It was like all those people who said, "call me if you need anything" after Caroline's funeral, none of them really meaning it. Still, he couldn't seem to help himself. Suddenly he needed to get out of the kitchen, get away from this disturbing connection he felt with Audrey.

"No, I'm fine. I'll be fine." Her smile was a heartbreaking lie.

"I'll take the…body…back with me if you want. You can't just leave it."

He watched her make up her mind. Literally, the decision to see this through played that clearly across her face. It tugged at him so strongly that a wave of panic flashed up his spine. "No," she said unsteadily. "I need to deal with this. You've done so much already." She reached across the huge gap between them—a few inches that felt like a canyon—and touched his arm. "I don't know how to thank you, Paul. Really."

He found himself unable to answer. Her touch shocked his mild panic into a blinding white dread. He managed a nod, some choking sort of grunt, and then let himself out the door.

He knew he should have stayed closer, offered more help during that next week, but he seemed unable to. Lilly went to Audrey's place every day after school, and he knew from the volunteers that she'd shortened her hours at the library, but something told him if he went near her, he wouldn't be able to handle it. It felt weak and cowardly.

He kept telling himself he was doing the wise thing, the safe thing for Lilly and him.

Yet, every night as he looked out and saw the light on in the barn, recognized the vigil she was keeping, he knew it was wrong.

Chapter Twelve

"They're here." Audrey nearly sang the words when Paul picked up the phone. "Two of the ewes gave birth overnight. I did it, Paul, they're here. Come look at them—four of them are here!"

It didn't matter that he had twelve other things he should be doing at that moment; the joy in her voice was irresistible.

Despite all his efforts to keep a distance over the last week, he would have gone out to her in a heartbeat. The week of distance had only brought him to one conclusion—he cared for her. The constant niggling in his chest wasn't the itch to run away from the vet practice; it was a craving to be near her. Not her sheep, *her*.

It had felt like a betrayal at first—some sort of crime against Caroline's memory—but during the week he'd realized his anxiety over Audrey's lambs was really a fear of his own "rebirth." They were connected, in one of those weird orchestrations only God creates; just as she needed the birth of the lambs to give a counterbalance to the loss of that first lamb, he could need what he felt for Audrey without taking anything away from what he felt for Caroline. At least that's how he understood it—it was more of a heart knowledge than any kind of logic he could ever hope to explain.

"Why didn't you call? I would have helped."

"It was the middle of the night. You couldn't have left Lilly. And it was okay. We were okay, Paul, the girls and I. The lambs are perfect—healthy and bonded to their mothers and absolutely beautiful. Come see!"

"Lilly got on the bus an hour ago. I'll be there in five minutes." He hadn't showered or shaved—he'd gotten a great writing idea at breakfast and he'd spent every moment since Lilly's departure at his computer. None of that mattered now—he didn't even bother with a coat, just threw on a pair of boots and pushed out the back door.

She was a wild, wide-eyed wonder this morning, running up to the fence to let him in when he could have easily opened the gate himself. "Paul, they're so wonderful. So amazing. Each of them. All of them!" Without hesitating, she grabbed his hand and pulled him toward the barn. And he let her, giving himself permission to be wrapped up in her joy this morning.

All the cuteness aside, newborn animals were always one of the best parts of Paul's vet practice. Something deep and powerful always settled in his chest as he witnessed life renew itself. Creation held such fantastic powers to soothe the soul; he could go through hours of a traumatic labor with an animal and still feel completely thrilled when the newborn stumbled up onto its legs for the first time. He knew—had always known—it was why God gave him Lilly to get through Caroline's departure. Youth and birth and growth were his touchstones, the things that energized him and renewed his faith.

He did not let go of her hand as they walked into the barn to view the morning's miracle. Mary and Esther had given birth, each to twins. The mothers and their babies were happily tucked into the individualized pens Audrey had set up.

He felt Audrey squeeze his hand, let his eyes fall shut for the briefest of moments as a long-lost pulse unwound in his chest. She'd done beautifully, and he was startled at the sense of pride that swelled inside him at the sight of the pairs of snowy, wobbly lambs.

"They're so beautiful," she said in an awed whisper. "I don't think I've ever seen anything so beautiful, ever." One of them looked up at her voice and bleated, a tiny, toy-sheep sound that made him smile and her laugh. Audrey pulled away from him to kneel down into one of the pens. A lamb bumbled over on its knobby legs to stare at her with adorable eyes. Of all God's newborns, lambs had to be among the most charming, all pink ears and black eyes and velvet noses. This particular velvet nose was bonking up against Audrey's arm, producing a giggle he felt tumble down the back of his spine. "Oh, look at her," she called back, her eyes big pools of wonder, charming him even more than the lamb's.

He crouched down beside her, smiling himself. "Actually, I think this is a little fella," he said as the black nose took a turn bumping up against him. "Hey there, little guy." Paul ran his hands expertly over the animal, assessing its overall health. He was in great shape. She'd done everything needed for the animals, and he knew that success would mean so much to her in light of Martha's stillborn birth. "You're looking just fine," he said to the lamb. "Happy birthday."

Audrey laughed, clearly taken with the idea. "It is, isn't it?" Audrey moved over to the other pen, singing "Happy Birthday" as she did. He let himself enjoy her voice, relish her delight, slightly startled at how happy *he* was. As he watched her move among the lambs, singing to them, he felt his heart unfold. He knew his own rebirth had begun. The thought—a ridiculously frilly thought for a man of his years and experience—rendered his legs as wobbly as the lambs' as he walked toward her.

His realization would show the minute she turned to him. He knew he'd be powerless to hide it—some part of him was that thirsty to care again. Why on earth had he tried to deny it?

When she finally turned, Paul thought his legs had given way. *Guys don't swoon,* he thought, feeling young and foolish. He was right; she felt it, as well. It showed instantly in that transparent face of hers. The gentlest of smiles curled up the corners of her mouth under lashes that were wet with tears. When was the last time he saw tears of joy? It seemed a tiny miracle, a wonder that stole his breath and lodged a lump in his own throat. "Oh, Paul," she said, walking toward him. "Everything's starting new, isn't it?"

She couldn't have picked words that would undo him more.

Audrey couldn't help but stare at Paul, wildly, acutely aware of what was transpiring between them. They weren't talking about the lambs anymore, and they both knew it. Especially when he choked out "They're amazing," without even looking at the animals. "I'm glad they're finally here."

She'd been so cautious, so hesitant. They'd drawn a careful line between them for so long. No longer. Audrey took a deep breath and forced herself to say, "I'm glad *you're* here." She wanted them to cross that line. She'd thought about him so much since that horrible morning with Martha's lamb and how tenderly he'd treated her. He'd stolen her heart that morning, but they'd pushed each other away. Why are human hearts so foolish when it matters most? Never mind—today was a day for new beginnings. Today was the day to start over. Or maybe just to start. She held his eyes until she thought her knees could go out from underneath her.

His smile came slowly, gaining ground as he closed the distance between them. "I am, too." Where had all the air suddenly gone? She realized, as he took yet another step, that hearts really did pound—it wasn't just a figure of speech. "I wasn't. Not at first. I kept so much distance between us."

"No." She rushed to contradict him. "You were careful." You were hurting, she wanted to say, but such negative words seemed wrong for the moment.

"Too careful. But you can be persistent, you know that?"

"About the lambs, maybe. But…" He was so close she couldn't finish the sentence. They were going to cross that line and there was no going back. She was terrifyingly happy, her breath coming in gulps as he reached up and brushed a piece of straw from her hair.

He didn't move his hand away. "You care," he corrected softly. "And thank God for that." His eyes told her he meant it.

"Paul," she said, wringing her hands. "You don't need to…"

"Shh." He moved his hand from her hair to place a single finger onto her lips. "I'm okay. Really." The finger moved from her lips to her cheek, a featherlight touch that would have stolen her heart if it had not already been his. In that moment, that excruciatingly long moment before he leaned his face toward her, Audrey thought him the most handsome, gentlest man God ever created. And when he kissed her, an exquisite, careful kiss that spoke of all he'd been through and all the future held, Audrey knew that hearts really did *burst* and people really did *fall* in love. She could have rolled every romantic cliché the library held into one long sentence and never come close to describing that kiss.

Her hands found their way to his shoulders, feeling the same sigh escape him that tumbled inside her. She could sense his discovery, taste the wonder in his deepening kiss. *Bliss* was the word that echoed through her mind as she tried to stay standing even though the barn seemed to be spinning around her.

Ruth bumped up against them, ending the kiss in a peal of laughter. "We've got chaperones," he chuckled, his eyes warm and joyful.

"Or matchmakers. My girls are very smart."

"They are," he agreed, threading his fingers through hers. "But you're going to need to switch to calling them 'your flock.' You've got rams now, not just ewes."

"And we all know what happens when you get rams and ewes together."

She didn't think his smile could get any broader. "Good things." He slipped his hands around her waist and kissed her forehead.

Audrey settled her head onto his shoulder and thought she might really die of happiness. "I want Lilly to help me name the lambs."

Paul pulled back to look at her. "She'll love that. But you might regret it."

"I said 'help.'" She feigned a stern expression. "I plan to retain full authority."

"Let me know how that works out for you," he said, laughing again. "I'm not sure I've ever succeeded at that."

Audrey reached out and swept a lock of hair from his eyes. "You're a wonderful father." She kissed his cheek, reveling in the texture of his face, the strength of his chin, the way his hair waved in certain places. He was such a good man. "How should we tell Lilly?"

"About us? Oh, she's even smarter than your girls. She'll figure it out soon enough." He raised an eyebrow. "The grinning dad is always a giveaway."

"Baaa." Martha and Mary echoed their agreement.

Chapter Thirteen

"I'm glad for the business, really I am," said Janet Bishop, who owned the hardware store, when Audrey stopped in the morning after Palm Sunday. "But I'll be glad when this parade craziness is over. I've had panicked people in here looking for gizmos to fix mistakes, people bickering over the last can of blue spray paint and Vern had to actually break up a fight between two guys over a tub of papier-mâché mix yesterday." She shut her cash register drawer with a weary thud. "Why is it Howard's ideas for town joy always result in king-size stress for the rest of us?"

Audrey didn't answer. She was feeling the crunch worse than anyone—or ought to have been by rights—but just couldn't muster up any misery lately. No one's complaints could make a dent in her happiness. Ruth had successfully delivered her lambs three days after Mary and Esther, which meant more sleepless nights, but even that failed to weary her. Howard's constant micromanagement couldn't get under her skin, which was probably why Janet was looking at her with a whopping dose of suspicion.

"Only our Parade Chair doesn't look too frazzled, even

with her new mouths to feed. Congratulations, by the way. All six delivered safe and sound?"

"Two rams, four ewes, all happy and healthy." Audrey's chest swelled with pride as she pulled the photos from her purse. "They're adorable, aren't they?"

"Cuties. But that smile goes a little deeper than Little Bo Peep finding her sheep if you ask me." Janet arched an eyebrow. "Rumor has it you get along *really well* with your neighbors."

Audrey shot Janet a shocked look.

"Second graders don't have a lot of tact, and Ms. Madison doesn't keep a secret very well. That, and the fact that you sat together at church on Sunday."

Audrey didn't know what to say. One second she was bursting to tell everyone the news, the next it felt fragile and private. She felt as though she should apologize for every judgmental thought she'd ever had about the crazy ways Janet, Emily and Dinah had all acted upon falling in love—she was surely worse then all of them put together.

Janet, who shared a practical nature closest to Audrey's, put an understanding hand on Audrey's arm. "I'm thrilled for you, really I am. Too long in coming, if you ask me."

Audrey felt as if her face turned five shades of red. "He's so wonderful. I'm just so flustered. I feel like an idiot."

"Well, you don't look like one. You look like a happy woman fixing to fall for the perfect guy." Janet pointed at Audrey with a ruler she pulled off the counter. "I knew God had someone special lined up for you one of these days."

"Speaking of days, I just hope I can hold up long enough to finish the last two final parade float inspections. I have to fit them in between shepherding tasks and, well, not everyone's been cooperative."

"Oh, I know," Janet said, putting a can of spray paint back

on the shelf. "The men's basketball league guy came in here all fired up last week because they'd been told to reinforce the backboard on their float."

"Cameron should know better," Audrey replied. "You can't just throw a portable basketball hoop up on someone's flatbed like that. It might fall over if the guy driving the truck stops too fast. Honestly, you'd think people's common sense flew out the window just because we said the word *parade*." She leaned in. "And what's basketball got to do with Easter, anyway?"

"If you ask Cameron and Dinah, basketball has something to do with everything. Did you know she wanted to put 'Hoopy Easter' on the side? Cameron only barely convinced her not to."

"Believe it or not—" Audrey raised an eyebrow "—I've seen worse." She checked her watch. "Gotta get back to the barn. The rest of that feed will be in on Tuesday, right?"

"Checked on the order yesterday. You're all set. Wouldn't want those mama sheep to go hungry now, would we?"

"No, ma'am." Audrey headed for the door, ticking through the list of errands still on her list.

"Oh, and Audrey?"

"Yes?"

"Hoopy Easter to you and your neighbors."

Paul stared at Sandy Burnside as they each ate a slice of pie at the diner. When she'd told him she had something important to talk to him about, he didn't know what to think. "Really?"

"Yes, I think it's a perfectly wonderful idea. But I wouldn't dream of asking her without your say-so."

"Why on earth would I object to Lilly being the Grand Marshal of Middleburg's Easter Parade? She'll go crazy at the idea."

"Well, I have to say I'd have been surprised if you refused, but you never know. Just seems to me, she's had a rough go of it losing her mama, and seeing as she's our newest and youngest citizen, well, it made all kinds of sense. My store'll fix her up with whatever new dress she'd like, and she'll get to ride on the back of Mac MacCarthy's snazzy little convertible at the head of the parade."

It sounded like the best Easter ever for a seven-and-three-quarters-year-old girl. God had indeed led him to the perfect new home for Lilly and him. "You should ask her yourself. I think she'd like that. She'll be home from school around three-thirty."

"I'll swing on by. Audrey wanted me to come by and see her new babies today, anyhow. And, of course, there you are *right next door.*" She said that last part with a broad hint of conspiracy. Maybe that small-town business about everybody knowing everything instantly was true. "Just works out perfectly, don't it?"

He didn't know what to say. Had the new relationship between him and Audrey been that obvious? Sandy could have been talking about his veterinary ability to help with the lambs, but it sure didn't look as if that's what she meant. Her eyes held a mischievous sparkle that left little to interpretation. "What do you mean?" he said slowly.

Her smile held such warmth. "Oh, now, we ain't so slow on the uptake as you might think. Besides, I like to see people happy. Especially ones that have seen as much sadness as you have. We're not meddling. We're just pleased to see two folks get together, that's all."

Paul gulped. "How many people know?"

She smirked. "Nearly everyone. I imagine choir practice tonight'll finish off the last few who don't know." Paul's worry for Audrey must have shown on his face, for Sandy reached out and patted his hand. "Audrey's dear to us. I'm just tickled

God's found the right man for her, and so's everybody else. Just be happy. That's all that's ever needed."

Good Friday had always been a difficult day. Even though Easter and Good Friday came on different days each year, Paul had always connected Caroline's death with Eastertime. Good Friday was such a somber, death-centered day, but Easter was the whole point of knowing Caroline's place in Heaven. It made Easter week a seesaw of emotions for Paul. Only this year, he didn't feel as tossed by emotional waves. He felt as if the whole process was coming full circle some-how, that the conflicting emotions were just two halves of the same whole.

Audrey sat with Paul and Lilly at the Good Friday service. She seemed to know, instinctively, what a fragile time this was for him. She didn't force him to talk much, waiting patiently for his comments to surface. It was a very good feeling to know she was there when he needed her. Never before had the phrase "Death hath lost its sting" been so real.

Lilly, on the other hand, talked a lot. After they sat having the now-traditional hot chocolate after the service, Paul was stunned to watch Lilly tell Audrey her version of the story of Caroline's death. Lilly told Audrey how Caroline had been sick and sad but that now because Jesus did the things He did she was having fun in Heaven. Her simple, trusting grasp of Easter's eternal truths astounded him.

"Do you think Martha's lamb is in Heaven? Meeting Mom?" Lilly asked.

Paul watched Audrey tear up but still smile. "I like that idea, don't you?" she choked out, her hand stealing to Paul's under the table.

"If he's as cute as all the other lambs, I bet they're having so much fun. Your lambs are fun. A lot of work, but fun." Lilly licked a dollop of whipped cream off her cocoa. "Are you gonna have more?"

"More lambs?" Audrey gasped, "Oh, no." A smile crept across her face. "I've got all I can handle between my Easter lambs and my Easter Lilly." With that she leaned over and planted an exquisitely tender kiss on Lilly's forehead while squeezing Paul's hand.

Paul's heart broke open and healed in the same wondrous instant. A fitting miracle for the time when the world broke open and healed on an eternal scale.

Chapter Fourteen

Easter could be a tricky business in Kentucky. April was mostly warm, but a cold rain could make springtime feel far away. Today was one of God's Saturday-morning master-pieces, a picture-perfect blue sky hosting fluffy clouds and brilliant sunshine. The most perfect day for an Easter Parade Audrey could ever imagine.

Sure, three floats had serious technical problems. The head had fallen off the Equestrian Club's float twice, so that now an unattractive contraption of chicken wire and duct tape held the horse's head on at a freakish angle. The riding-mower-brigade noise had sent the kennel club's dogs into a barking hysteria, necessitating a last-minute reordering of four floats. One of the 4-H goats had munched off a corner of the high school glee club float. Still, Ballad Road was awash in pastel streamers and balloons, and even the crudest float glowed in the bath of sunshine God had given the world.

Paul and Lilly had come over to the church parking lot hours before the parade, bringing Audrey tea and muffins. It felt so very lovely to be "tended to" that it evaporated most of the stress right out of Audrey's body. Yes, details had gone awry, but the important things were in place. The important people, too.

The attraction she felt for Paul had felt like a loss of control at first. Another layer in an already too-layered life. She'd realized, in the days since the lambs had come, that what she felt for Paul was a *foundation,* not a distraction. It gave her the grounding that enabled her to ebb and flow with life's changes. Yes, faith had always given that to her, but needing Paul would never mean needing God less. Just loving more.

And loving Paul had meant loving Lilly, too. Lilly, who brought light and joy right alongside her commotion and craziness. Easter was so much more wonderful with Lilly and Paul to share it. It gave her enormous pleasure to make sure what she'd come to think of as "Lilly's Parade" would go off without a hitch.

Or, as she had now learned to expect, without *too many* hitches.

The now-familiar surge of affection for Paul and Lilly warmed her all over again, and Audrey looked up from her clipboard to scan the parking lot for the pair. There, standing next to Mac MacCarthy's shiny orange convertible, was its VIP occupant and her father. Paul looked charmed if a little overwhelmed by it all as he settled Lilly in for her Grand Marshal ride. Lilly, however, drank in the day for all it was worth. She wore a rose-colored dress with cream trim, a tone that showed off her hair and complexion to great advantage. Sandy knew her stuff. Just frilly enough to be dramatic, but not too much. Lilly looked like a princess, which is exactly how she should have looked. And felt.

Pastor Anderson said a blessing over the parade floats and groups as they lined up in the church parking lot. It was the one still moment in a morning chock-full of last-minute hysteria for Audrey. As he finished, he handed the microphone to Lilly. With a beaming smile, she called out "Let the Parade begin" just the way they'd rehearsed. Behind her, Paul's smile was nearly as broad as his daughter's. Audrey felt the warmth of his expression just as surely as she felt the sun on her face.

As she raised her clipboard, ready to tick off the parade entrants as they went by, a set of hands removed it from her grasp. "You've got better things to do," Janet said as she pulled a pencil from behind her ear.

"What do you mean by that?"

She looked over to see Paul extending his hand to her. "Go take a walk, Audrey," Janet said. "You've earned it."

"You mean...? I couldn't."

Janet shrugged. "You could. You should. Besides," she said, pushing Audrey toward Paul's place behind the orange car, "I'm not giving this clipboard back. *Doctor's* orders."

Paul grinned. Janet nudged Audrey again. "C'mon!" Lilly yelled as Mac moved the convertible slowly forward. "Dad's been waiting forever."

So had she. Audrey took the hand of the man she'd come to love, and together, they stepped off in the first-ever Annual Middleburg Easter Parade.

* * * * *

Dear Reader,

I love yarn and knitting, so it's no surprise sheep would show up eventually. I was unprepared, however, for the many lessons and insights these animals gave. God wisely uses many metaphors of sheep and flocks—they have a startling amount to teach us about faith, trust and community.

Got has given you—yes, you—unique gifts and qualities to share with your community. Sometimes we need to redefine "community," or redefine what we consider "gifts." Why? Because God hides surprises and blessings in places we often consider empty. These are challenging times, but when we remember that God is mightier than any challenge, His glory enables amazing things. Therein lies the most beautiful qualities of the Body of Christ.

Tend to your own flock—whatever its shape and size— with care and creativity. God is just waiting to astound you when you do. As always, I love to hear from you at aliepleiter.com or P.O. Box 7026, Villa Park, IL 60181.

QUESTIONS FOR DISCUSSION

1. Can you think of a time when life exploded beyond your capacity to cope? What did God show you during that time?

2. Do you have a gift, like Audrey's knitting, that you can share? Why or why haven't you shared it? If there are opportunities to use that gift right in front of you now, what can you do?

3. Do you agree with Paul's decision to move to Middleburg? When is a fresh start a good thing? Is it ever a poor choice?

4. Would you have been in favor of Howard's Easter Parade idea? Why or why not?

5. Where do the Easter themes of redemption and restoration show up most strongly for you in the story? Why?

*When his niece unexpectedly arrives at his Montana ranch,
Jules Parrish has no idea what to do with her—or with
Olivia Rose, the pretty teacher who brought her.
Will they be able to build a life—and family—together?*

*Here's a sneak peek of "Montana Rose"
by Cheryl St.John,
one of the touching stories in the new collection,
TO BE A MOTHER,
available April 2010
from Love Inspired Historical.*

Jules Parrish squinted from beneath his hat brim, certain the
waves of heat were playing with his eyes. Two females—one
a woman, the other a child—stood as he approached.

The woman walked toward him. Jules dismounted and approached her. "What are you doing here?"

The woman stopped several feet away. "Mr. Parrish?"

"Yeah, who are you?"

"I'm Olivia Rose. I was an instructor at the Hedward Girls
Academy." She glanced back over her shoulder at the girl who
watched them. "My young charge is Emily Sadler, the
daughter of Meriel Sadler."

She had his attention now. He hadn't heard his sister's
name in years. *Meriel.*

"The academy was forced to close. I thought Emily should
be with family. You're the only family she has, so I brought
her to you."

He took off his hat and raked his fingers through dark,

wavy hair. "Lady, I spend every waking hour working horses and cows. I sleep in a one-room cabin. I don't know anything about kids—and especially not girls."

"What do you suggest?"

"I don't know. All I know is, she can't stay here."

*Will Olivia be able to change Jules's mind
and find a home for Emily—and herself?*

*Find out in
TO BE A MOTHER,
the heartwarming anthology from
Cheryl St.John and Ruth Axtell Morren,
available April 2010
only from Love Inspired Historical.*